Remember My Name

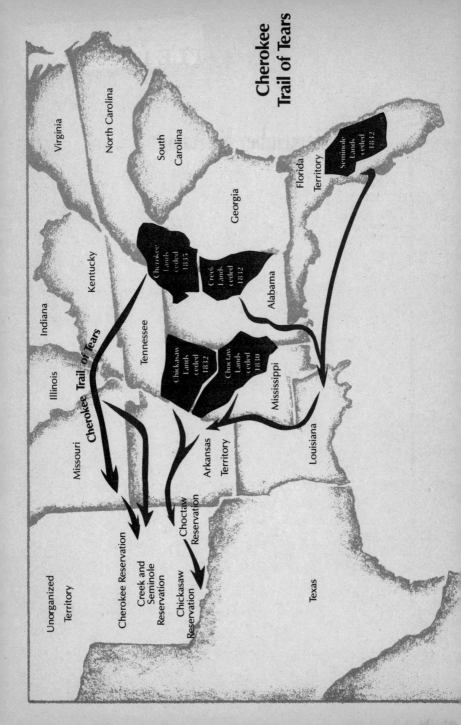

Remember My Name

Sara H. Banks

**Illustrations
by Birgitta Saflund**

SCHOLASTIC INC.
New York Toronto London Auckland Sydney

For my son and his son,

and for those yet unborn of the *Ani' Yun' wiya'*, "whose faces are coming from beneath the ground."

ISBN 0-590-22500-6

Copyright © 1993 by Sara H. Banks. All rights reserved. Published by Scholastic Inc., 555 Broadway, New York, NY 10012, by arrangement with Roberts Rinehart Publishers.

12 11 10 9 8 7 6 5 4 3 2   5 6 7 8 9/9 0/0

Printed in the U.S.A.   40

First Scholastic printing, March 1995

Contents

Acknowledgments

I am indebted to James Mooney, whose monumental works, the seventh and nineteenth *Annual Reports for the Bureau of America Ethnology,* documented and preserved the history of the Cherokee people. His *Historical Sketch of the Cherokee* is the lodestone by which the path of this history is charted. Another whose expertise I depended on was Samuel Carter III, in his scholarly *Cherokee Sunset: A Nation Betrayed.* I would also like to thank Hap Gilliland, who believed in *Remember My Name,* and Carrie Jenkins, at Roberts Rinehart, whose understanding allowed me to improve and strengthen this book. And, to my friend Harriet Kelley, who never stopped believing in me, a debt of gratitude.

"If we had no lands, we should have fewer enemies."

—Old Tassell,
Chief of the Cherokees at Echota, in 1792

". . . the Cherokee removal was the cruelest work I ever knew."

—Private John G. Burnett, from his papers,
written a half century after the Indian Removal of 1838

Chapter One

The Sunflower Room

Annie sat on the cabin steps alone. Her long dark skirt was tucked around her knees as she chewed absently on the end of her glossy braid that was the dark brown of a horse chestnut. From the lilac bushes in the yard, a mockingbird sang a joyful song. She looked over at him and sighed deeply. He sounded much too happy for such a sad day.

It was September and the fields were still green. Down in the meadow, sunflowers grew tall, their bright yellow heads following the path to the sun. Annie was waiting for her uncle William Blackfeather. She wondered what he'd look like. Although he was a full-blood, like her mother, he might have changed since the last time she saw him. That had been five years ago, when she was six years old. He was her mother's brother and lived at New Echota, the Cherokee capital of the Nation. Now he was coming to Star Mountain to take her back with him. And she wasn't at all sure that she wanted to go. In fact, she was pretty sure that she didn't. But no one had asked what she wanted.

"I still don't see why I have to go," she muttered to no one in particular. "I could stay here and live with *Na-nye'hi*. She can teach me everything I need to know. I don't need to go to school."

Everything was wrong somehow. For a moment, the blackness that sometimes fell over her seemed about to happen. Her parents were . . . the word drifted in and she pushed it away. She couldn't even *think* the word. They were gone . . . but the word pushed its way into her head. They were dead. Something gripped her heart with a fierceness that made her catch her breath. They were gone. And she missed them so.

A soft footfall sounded behind her and she turned. Her grandmother, *Nanye'hi*, stood in the doorway.

"It's time, little one," she said, holding out her hand. "Your uncle will be here soon."

Nanye'hi was tall and thin and wore the traditional Indian dress of a buckskin shift and soft boots. Her hair, sprinkled with gray, was worn in two long braids. Taking her grandmother's hand, Annie asked, "How do you know? How do you know he's coming now?"

"The mockingbird, *Conconolatally*, told me with one of his four hundred tongues," replied Nanye'hi. "Come now, *Agin'agili*," she said, using Annie's Cherokee name. "You must be ready when my son William comes to fetch you."

"We must use my other name," whispered Annie. But her grandmother paid no attention to her. "Come," she said.

When she was six, Annie had discovered a place where sunflowers grew in a kind of natural square, the bright yellow blossoms always turning towards the sun. Taller than her head, the stalks had offered shade on a hot afternoon when she'd been waiting for her mother, who was picking blackberries in the sunlit field. Hot and sleepy, Annie had wandered off into the cool green shelter of the flowers.

Hours later, Annie was found asleep in what soon became her favorite place. Each year after that, Annie's father had planted sunflowers so that they grew in a square, and when they were higher than her head, her mother had woven leaves and branches through them, making a small room, a private place just for Annie. The day before yesterday, Annie had gone down to the meadow, to her secret place.

Slipping through the narrow opening in the wall of green, she had entered her sunflower room. From the deep pocket of her shift, she took out her favorite doll and laid it gently on the ground. The doll's features, once brightly painted, were blurred and faint from much loving. Her dress of deerskin was worn soft as silk and the feather in her hair was bedraggled and wispy.

Reaching up, Annie tore off a broad leaf from a sunflower stalk and wrapped it around her doll like a shawl. Then, with a sharp stick, she began digging a hole. When she'd finished, she laid the doll inside and covered her with earth.

"I'm too old for you now," she said softly. "And now you are buried here with my name. Where I am going, I will be called Annie Stuart. No one will remember my Cherokee name."

The world she was entering would be a different world from the one she had known on Star Mountain. No one had told her this, but she knew, just the same. Nothing would ever be the same again.

And so, *Agin'agili* buried her doll along with her name and turned her back on her secret place.

Chapter Two

The Darkening Land

Annie was packing her things when she heard the muffled sound of hoofbeats on the path leading to the cabin. She ran into the front room and looked out. A lone rider appeared beneath the tall trees. He was riding a chestnut stallion whose coat gleamed in the patches of sunlight that filtered through the tops of the trees. She watched as he dismounted and walked up the front steps.

He was tall and wore buckskin trousers and shirt. His hair was cut in the shorter fashion of the whites and was black as a crow's wing. When he saw Annie at the window, he smiled. Surprised, she saw that it looked like her mother's smile. She went to the door to greet him.

"Well, Annie Rising Fawn Stuart," said William Blackfeather. "We meet again. You were only six years old when I last saw you." He lifted her chin with one finger and looked long into her face, at her wide-set eyes that were the gray of mountain mist, at her high cheekbones. "You look like your mother," he said. "You're a fair one, Annie. Your parents did you proud."

Then he greeted his mother lovingly and when Annie saw them together she felt better than she had for a long time. The weight that had been on her heart lifted a tiny bit for the first time since the death of her parents.

A little while later, Annie left the cabin to say her goodbyes to the animals on the place. Beech leaves were scattered like gold coins over the damp earth as she walked up to the upper meadow where the sheepbarn stood, its outline softened by mists. At twilight, the sheep stood huddled close together, their curly wool glistening with the fine rain that had begun early in the afternoon. They were Dorsets, with white faces and pure white wool. Annie told each one goodbye, touching the shaggy roughness of their damp fleece.

"I'll be back," she whispered, touching their soft ears. "Somehow, I'll come. Remember me."

From the meadow, she walked back through the soft rain and climbed to the top of the cliff behind the cabin. There was scarcely a sound except the faint pattering of rain on the leaves. The silence wrapped around her like a cloak and she had the feeling that there, in the stillness of the woods, where the earth was rich and dark, that she could put her finger to the earth and feel it throbbing beneath her touch like the heart of a bird.

Then, from the shelter of the trees, a young doe appeared, almost as if Annie had wished her there. She moved so lightly that she seemed barely to touch the ground. Pausing, she sniffed the air, and, raising a slender leg, looked over at Annie. Her eyes were dark and liquid and seemed to Annie to hold all the secrets of the world. Annie caught her breath, scarcely daring to breathe and for an instant, they gazed at one another. Then, with a bound as effortless as smoke, the doe whirled and disappeared back into the forest. When she'd gone, Annie walked over to where she'd been. The delicate hoofprints were silver-rimmed in the wet grass.

"Farewell," Annie whispered, "farewell."

That night, *Nanye'hi* prepared a supper of fresh fish, hot cornbread and stewed apples. And after they had eaten, the three of them sat in front of the fire. *Nanye'hi* smoked her pipe, the bowl of which was carved of red stone, in the shape of a raven. *Nanye'hi* had told Annie that the stone was sacred, and that in the past, their people had traveled hundreds of miles to a far-away place to get the stone from sacred caves; caves that were known but to few.

Taking a puff of the pipe, *Nanye'hi* blew fragrant smoke into the four corners of the room; north, east, south, and west: the four corners of the earth. She called on the spirits of the Grandfathers.

The spirits were holy and she asked them for wisdom and courage. And when the ritual was over, she asked her son,

"Do you still practice the old ways of our people?"

He nodded. "The Supreme Being is called by different names by different people," he said. "But while my wife is a Christian, we still hold the same beliefs in many things."

The cabin was warm and rosy with firelight. The smell of applewood was sweet and mingled with the scent of tobacco. Annie listened sleepily to the voices of her grandmother and her uncle. In a few minutes she got up, and going over to a peg on the wall, took down her father's old plaid shawl. He had told her that the tartan, as it was called, showed by its design and plaid that he was a Scot who belonged to the Stuart Clan. He had been proud of his clan and of his own people. Wrapping herself in the soft woolen tartan, Annie curled up in the rocking chair and closed her eyes.

Nanye'hi spoke, her words circling like moths in the quiet room. "I have read the bones," she said, "and I have heard the voices of the Grandfathers in the smoke of the sacred pipe. They tell me of a great evil that will come to our people. A fierce wind will sweep over the lands of the Cherokee, the *Ani yun wiya*, killing and scattering us to the four corners of the earth. Like leaves, they will be blown to the north, which is dark and stormy, and to the west; to *Usunhi'yi*, the 'darkening land'."

Uncle William made a low noise in his throat. "It isn't going to happen," he said. "It's true that there are men in power in this country who wish to take our lands, the lands that have belonged to our people since the beginning. But it won't happen. Even now, John Ross, our chief, is in Washington speaking for our people."

Nanye'hi gazed into the fire. Her eyes were hooded and dark and in the firelight, she wore the look of an eagle.

"Know this, William Blackfeather," she said. "The time will come when our people will be locked in cages like animals. You will see this come to pass. But this child, my little *Agin'agili*, is a child of the mountains, a child of the mists. She must remain free. Remember that! She must remain free!"

William glanced behind him to see if Annie slept. He was afraid she might be frightened by his mother's talk. When he turned back, *Nanye'hi* had closed her eyes and appeared to sleep, sitting in her usual place by the fire. Her long fingers closed inward like the claws of a great bird. William was silent.

Getting up, he added a log to the fire. The Cherokees were threatened on all sides. The whites wanted the rich lands that belonged to the Indians. And gradually, they were getting what they wanted, through broken treaties and lies. And the government allowed it to happen. It was a thing too big to understand. But at the root of it was greed; a greed that ruined lives and took away a people's pride.

Many Indians believed in certain ideas. One was that land and its produce, like air and water, were not to be owned, but shared. No man could own land and keep others from it. A tribe could claim certain land for farming, or living on, but it was for the use of all. Some tribes regarded the earth as the mother of all life and thought it impossible to sell their mother. This belief caused trouble between the Indians and the whites. William was worried. Some bad things had already happened. But he believed it would get better. It had to.

Gradually the fire died down and the last log broke with a soft rustle. The coals glowed briefly, then turned to ash. For the first time, the fire was allowed to die in the fireplace. There would be no need of the morning's flames to begin the day. The cabin would be empty of life and would hold only memories. *Nanye'hi* would return to the small Cherokee village hidden away in the mountains. Although William had asked her to return with him to New Echota, she had refused. She'd never leave her beloved mountains, she'd said, "Never."

A little while later, Annie felt herself being lifted in strong arms and taken gently to her own room in the loft.

"Good night, Annie," said her uncle. "Things will get better." Then he closed the door and Annie was left alone.

The barn owl soared soundlessly in the night, his creamy feathers silvered by moonlight. He flew from his perch in the rafters of the barn, across the meadows and through the trees to the cabin. Uttering a low, "shiiish," he perched in the pine tree near Annie's window.

Annie heard his soft cry. She turned to the window and looked out at the night sky that was starred and shining. She'd been born on Star Mountain and it was the only home she'd ever known. Now, she had to leave. Closing her eyes tightly, she pulled the quilt over her head.

"Don't call my name," she whispered in the night. Everyone knew that to hear an owl call your name meant that something awful would happen to you.

"Go away," she said, "fly away, *u'guku*, fly away."

The owl looked out over the small patch of garden, his monkey-face white and heart-shaped. He saw nothing to interest him; the mice were hidden. Once again, he flew silently through the branches, his wings ghostly and pale.

Chapter Three

The Trembling Hills

The morning stars were blooming when Annie first opened her eyes. Dressing quickly, she went into the main room of the cabin to find her grandmother. The room was silent and still and seemed wrapped in mist.

"*Nanye'hi*?" she called. "Where are you?"

But there was no answer. Her grandmother had gone. Her blanket, pipe, basket of herbs and bones; all were gone. Annie sat down on the hearth where last night's ashes were cold and powdery. She shivered slightly in the dampness. Then she saw the small deerskin pouch at the side of the fireplace. It was the bag in which *Nanye'hi* had kept the magic rock.

Taking the bag over to the table, Annie lit the lamp and carefully took the rock out of the bag. The rock was heavy in her palm and glittered with tiny specks in the lamplight. Many times, she had watched her grandmother turn the rock over and over in her hands, lifting it to catch the firelight, turning it to capture the sun.

Nanye'hi had many powers. She was a "Beloved Woman" in the tribe. She sat in the councils and was considered wise. And while she had never said that the rock was magic, Annie knew somehow that it was special. Turning it over in her hands, Annie wished that *Nanye'hi* had told her how to use it. She figured that only her grandmother knew its powers. But *Nanye'hi* was gone and had left the stone for Annie.

She replaced the rock in its pouch and looked around the room. Her mother's loom sat near the fireplace. Nearby sat her own stool, carved out of a single piece of wood by her father. His dulcimer hung on a peg on the wall. When he played the Scottish tunes he loved, plucking the strings lightly, the music was like water over rocks or wind in the trees. "Can you smell the heather, lass?" he'd say.

A rag rug hid the place in the floor where there was a trap door leading down to the root cellar where her mother stored dried apples and meats, honey and cornmeal. Now, the loom was empty of bright wool and the dulcimer was stilled. . . .

"Annie," called her uncle from the porch. "It's time to go."

Wasps droned over windfall apples that had fallen to the ground. Muscadines, the wild sweet grapes, hung in dusky clusters on the arbor as Annie joined her uncle. As she said her last goodbye to the place she loved, she felt as though she were made of glass and that if she moved too quickly, she would break and shatter into a thousand pieces.

When they had mounted their horses and were ready to go, Uncle William turned to her. "You've a hard path to travel," he said. "Two more independent people than Cherokees and Highlanders never walked this earth. And you are a part of each and both of them. You'll follow the windpath and heed the call of the mountains, Annie. But you may pay a dear price for it." He smiled as if to make his words easier to hear.

"I believe you have a lot of common sense. That will help." He patted the muzzle of his horse then said,

"Your father had a word for common sense . . . a Scottish word. . . ."

Annie looked at him. "Rumblegumption," she said, a smile barely passing over her face.

"What?" he asked.

"That's what my father used to call common sense."

"Good word," said Uncle William as he turned his horse and started down the mountain path. "A very good word."

The air was crisp and a rich scent of leafmold and crushed leaves filled Annie's nostrils. They moved in single-file down the path, called by the mountain people, a "trace." Their way at first was shadowy, then, on the other side of the mountain, they rode into the sun. As it rose above the tallest mountain, it filled the valley with gold and poured broad bands of shining rays into the dark hollows and coves, bringing brilliant color to the trees that shone red and scarlet and bronze. In the distance, the far mountains were wrapped in mist, like smoke. Uncle William reined in his horse and looked out over the glory that lay before them.

"Do you know the Psalms, Annie?" he asked.

" 'He looketh on the earth, and it trembleth;
He touches the hills, and they smoke'."

Then looking over at Annie he said, "Our people call these hills 'the trembling hills'."

And as Annie looked out over the valley and toward the distant mountains, she knew that she would never see anything lovelier. Then, turning her horse, she followed her uncle down the mountain.

That night, they stayed in the small village of *I'tawa*. The next morning, they took the Warrior Path through the foothills and into the great Southern forest. The year was 1835. It was a year that the Cherokees would remember forever with grief. It was the beginning of the end of the Cherokee Nation. *Nanye'hi*'s warnings would be remembered. And Annie would be a part of all that happened.

Chapter Four

Children of the Night

Uncle William reined in his horse and motioned Annie to do the same. "We'll camp here for the night," he said.

At the edge of the forest, the air blew cool out of the dense shade. Pine trees sighed in the wind. Annie listened to the sounds of the woods; a bobcat's scream, water tumbling over rocks, the music of a thousand birds. Ahead of them, a long avenue of trees grew as straight as though planted to form a street. At the end of this avenue, grassy banks rose to a hill; a kind of mound. Trees grew on top of the mound.

"What is this place?" asked Annie.

"It's called a *tallahassee*," replied her uncle. "It's an ancient place, a burial place of our ancestors."

The deep silence of the *tallahassee* seemed to press against Annie's ears

"Why did they leave?" she asked. "Why would our people leave this place and where did they go?"

"Sometimes they left because the fields were worn out with planting, or perhaps there was sickness in the village. Sometimes they left to join another tribe for safety."

"I don't think I like this place," said Annie, looking over her shoulder.

"There is nothing to fear here," said Uncle William. "Our people sleep peacefully. We'll stay the night on the mound where it is high and safe."

That night, after they had eaten a meal of freshly caught fish and the hard bread that *Nanye'hi* had baked and strung on a rawhide cord, they slept on the mound where the ancient dead were buried. They heard the cries of the black wolves, "the children of the night," that called in the loneliness of starlight.

The land began to flatten and there were fewer hills as they made their way to New Echota. At mid-morning, Annie said, "I smell the river." And sure enough, they soon approached the river at the ferry crossing.

The dock was noisy with the squeals of pigs and the cackle of hens. Crates of chickens were stacked and waiting and there were more people than Annie had ever seen in one place at one time. There were Indians, settlers, women with packages, soldiers, and farmers. Nearby, piraguas—small boats rowed by Cherokee oarsmen—were moored, awaiting passengers. Children ran about, yelling in shrill voices while their mothers tried to control them without much success. Annie and Uncle William ate their noon meal at a nearby inn and, afterwards, Uncle William bought Annie a sack of rock candy, which she tucked into her saddlebag.

The moon was covered by clouds when Annie and Uncle William finally reached the darkened streets of New Echota. Annie was so tired that she rode with her eyes closed, trusting her horse to deliver her safely. Through a fog, she heard her uncle say,

"We're home, Annie." But she didn't remember being taken off her horse and carried to her bed.

A rooster crowed at first light and Annie opened her eyes sleepily. She was in a room with white walls and shuttered windows. A plain wooden chest stood against one wall. On the chest were a flower-sprigged bowl and pitcher. Through the windows, she saw tree tops, the underside of the leaves reflecting the light.

Slipping out of bed, she tiptoed over to the window and opened the shutters wide. It was the first time she'd ever been in a two-story house and she felt as though she were in the tree tops. She looked down at gardens and carefully swept walkways. Woodsmoke hung in the air and mingled with another wonderful smell, the scent of freshly-baked bread rising from somewhere below the stairs.

Downstairs, she wandered around until she found her uncle sitting at a table with a lady who Annie thought was the sleekest person she'd ever seen. Her hair was brown and smoothed back in two wings over her ears. Her gown of black was equally smooth with only a black onyx brooch at the neck for decoration. She looked up as Annie came into the room.

Uncle William turned around in his chair. "Ah, Annie," he said, holding out his hand. "Come meet your Aunt Martha."

Aunt Martha smiled, but only slightly. Reaching over, Uncle William tweaked Annie's long braid. "Sit down and have some breakfast," he said. "After you've eaten, you can become acquainted with the house and the grounds and the animals."

"She can't eat in her nightgown," said Aunt Martha. "It isn't seemly."

Annie was embarrassed and turned to leave, but her uncle said, "Just for today, Martha. Come, Annie. Sit down. Charity will fetch your breakfast."

Before she could ask who Charity was, a black woman entered the dining room carrying a small tray on which was a bowl of hot, steaming cornmeal mush. She placed the bowl in front of Annie.

Annie had never seen a black person before and she stared at Charity, whose scarlet gown billowed softly around her bare ankles. She wore a white cloth wrapped around her head in a turban. Her eyes were dark, with heavy lids and her skin shone with a soft glow, like the bloom on a grape. Annie wanted to reach out and touch her, but didn't dare.

Charity didn't speak, but placed the food in front of Annie and left the room. Annie looked down. She hated cornmeal mush! She figured that nothing called "mush" could be good to eat, otherwise it would be called something else. She took a sip of tea, then nibbled on a biscuit, hoping that her aunt wouldn't notice that she wasn't eating the mush.

In a little while, Charity came back into the room. She looked at Annie, then looked at the still-full bowl but didn't say anything as she removed it. Annie breathed a sigh of relief.

"Why is she so dark?" she asked, watching Charity walk away, her back straight, her gown moving softly around her ankles.

"Charity is a slave and comes from Africa," replied her aunt. "Now, finish your breakfast, Annie. We've a lot to do this morning."

Where was Africa, Annie wondered, and was everyone from there a slave? And were they all dark, like Charity? But she didn't ask. Aunt Martha didn't look as though she wanted to hear any more questions.

Annie followed her aunt back upstairs. In her room, she glanced around. "Where are my things?" she asked.

"I've put them away," replied Aunt Martha. "You won't need them here."

"But I want them," Annie said. "They're mine. My mother made the coverlet out of turkey feathers. And I need my father's shawl and my rock."

"We'll see about them later," said Aunt Martha firmly. "First though, I want you to bathe, then we'll see about getting you into some decent clothes."

Annie wondered what was wrong with her own clothes. But she didn't say anything. She just waited while her aunt went over to the small chest where she poured water into the bowl from the pitcher. Then Aunt Martha handed her a small linen cloth. "Bathe well, Annie," she said. "I'll check your ears when you've finished."

Annie looked at the cloth, then at the bowl. Surely she wasn't expected to bathe in that little bit of water. But since that was the only water around, she probably was. She waited until her aunt was out of the room to begin. Bathing in a bowl was not nearly so nice as swimming in a clear creek where tiny silver fish nibbled your toes while birds sang overhead. People in town sure did things the hard way.

In a little while, Aunt Martha returned with an armful of clothes which she laid out on Annie's bed. There were linen petticoats, long ruffled drawers, stockings, and a dress of soft blue flax. "Try this on," she said, handing the dress to Annie. "It belonged to a girl who stayed with us while she attended the mission school. If it fits, I'll use it to make a pattern for other dresses for you. You can't wear deerskin shifts here in town."

When she was finally dressed, Annie felt as though she'd been stuffed. Her hair was braided into two plaits and tied with ribbon. The dress was long and had a high neck that she felt was going to choke the life out of her. The shoes were just plain awful. Annie couldn't believe she was expected to wear them. But from the look on her aunt's face, yes, that was just what she was to do.

"Walk over to the looking glass," said her aunt.

Annie's feet felt so heavy that she could barely move. The high-topped shoes were not at all like the soft moccasins that she'd always worn. She looked at herself in the glass. The girl in the looking glass looked taller and thinner in her long dress and funny shoes.

"Pick up your feet, Annie!" admonished her aunt, as she led the way out of the room. "Walk like a lady."

As she followed her aunt down the stairs, Annie wondered about what her aunt had said. "Walk like a lady?" Did ladies walk differently from other people? It was all very confusing.

Later that day, at twilight, Annie went back to her room. She saw that someone had put her shawl over the chair and her mother's coverlet was on the foot of the bed with the small deerskin pouch containing the rock. She rubbed her hands over the soft feathers of the coverlet. Her mother had spent an entire winter making it, first making a fine net of the inner fibers of the mulberry trees, then weaving glossy turkey feathers into a pattern of shining colors. She missed her mother. And she wanted to go home.

There was a soft knock at the door. Charity stood on the threshhold. Peeking out from under the hem of her skirt was a tiny gray kitten. When it opened its mouth, only the tiniest sound emerged, more like a squeak than a cry.

"I thought you might be needing some comfort," said Charity, handing Annie the kitten.

Annie buried her face in the soft, milky-scented fur, hiding her eyes that suddenly filled with tears. How could Charity have known that she'd be feeling so homesick, so awful?

"Thank you," she said softly.

A few days later, the household was assembled in the dining room for evening prayer. Annie was kneeling next to her chair, her eyes shut tight. A fly buzzed near her ear. Slapping at it, she nearly overturned the chair. When prayers ended, she opened her eyes to see Aunt Martha giving her a dark look.

"Annie," she said firmly, "It isn't seemly to wriggle during prayers. We have to show the proper respect."

"Yes'm," said Annie, not even sure what "proper respect" was. It did seem that she always managed to do the wrong thing when she was around Aunt Martha.

Uncle William served the chicken and cornbread and Aunt Martha passed a bowl of ginger apples and raisins. Firelight dappled the walls of the big room and cast deep shadows in the corners. Out of the corner of her eye, Annie saw a slight movement near the hearth. In the shadows, a young girl sat on a stool near the fire. Her head was in profile, her eyes lowered. She wore a long cotton dress and over it, a white apron that covered her from her shoulders to the hem of her dress. Her black hair was tightly braided into cornrows and showed a softly rounded forehead and an upturned nose. She looked to be about Annie's age. Glancing quickly over at Annie, she smiled, showing deep dimples in her cheeks.

Aunt Martha, following Annie's glance, said, "That's Righteous Cry. She's Charity's child. She's been helping out at Miss Olivia's house, down the road. Miss Olivia has been poorly and she needed someone."

"Why doesn't she eat with us?" Annie asked.

Aunt Martha's forehead creased in annoyance. "Because she's a slave," she said.

"Don't slaves eat?" asked Annie innocently.

"Please stop asking foolish questions and eat your supper," said Aunt Martha sharply.

Annie decided that people who lived in towns were really strange. She'd never even heard of slaves back on Star Mountain. *Nanye'hi* had told her stories about famous battles between tribes when slaves were taken, but that had been a long time ago, in the olden days. Why were Charity and Righteous Cry slaves, anyway? Had they been taken in battle? Were the other black people on the plantation slaves? She looked over at her uncle who was quietly eating his supper. He didn't look like a warrior, yet he had slaves. She wanted to ask more about it, but didn't dare. Aunt Martha was looking very stern.

The next day, Righteous showed Annie around the plantation. They went out to the fields where the outbuildings were. There were barns, a winnowing shed where wheat was threshed, a smoke house where meats were cured, and a tobacco barn. There was a springhouse where a stream bubbled merrily and where you could drink cold water from a dried gourd. Then they walked out to where there was a row of small wooden cabins.

"That's where we live," said Righteous, pointing to a cabin that sat in the shade of a chinaberry tree whose branches were filled with golden berries. "My mama and me live there. All the slaves lives out here but my mama and me, we live together."

Annie felt funny when Righteous talked about being a slave. It seemed wrong to her. She wondered if Righteous minded. When they left the cabins, Righteous asked, "You want to see my goat?"

A creek ran through the meadow behind the barn. They walked through the meadow and at the edge of the creek, a nanny goat was cropping grass. She was white and had yellow eyes. The goat watched as they approached, a bit of clover sticking out of one side of her mouth.

Righteous went over and began scratching the goat behind her ears. As she scratched, the goat began chewing on the hem of Righteous's dress. Righteous explained how Uncle William had given her the kid to raise.

"Her own mama wouldn't feed her," said Righteous. "So I gave her a bottle my mama fixed for me. She don't pay no mind to the other goats," she said, rescuing the hem of her dress. "I reckon she figures I'm her mama now."

"What's her name?" asked Annie.

"Joshua," said Righteous.

"Joshua?" said Annie. "How can her name be Joshua? That's a boy's name."

"Don't care," said Righteous, again pulling her skirt away from Joshua. "Joshua is my favorite name and *this* goat's name is Joshua."

Annie shrugged. "Well," she said, "she's your goat and I reckon you can name her anything you want."

"That's right," said Righteous. "I reckon I can."

Joshua followed them back to the garden gate behind the house. Annie's new kitten, which she'd named Rumblegumption, came out to greet them. Then, Rumblegumption saw Joshua. She slowed her steps, her tail held high in the air. She took a few sideways steps, dancing up to the goat as though she was square-dancing in the grass. Then, apparently deciding that goats were safe, she sat down at Joshua's feet and began washing her paws daintily as though meeting a goat was an everyday occurrence.

Then the girls walked over to where Charity was working in the garden, her back broad and strong as she searched for sweet potatoes.

"Righteous," she said, when the girls were even with her, "Go fetch a basket and get me some onions. Mind you gets small ones. Mr. William don't like 'em big."

As Annie helped Righteous dig for onions, she asked, "How come you're named Righteous Cry?"

"What?" asked Righteous, wiping dirt off the onions and putting them into the basket.

"Where does your name come from?" asked Annie.

"My mama give it to me," said Righteous. "It's from the Bible."

Charity overheard the question. "'The righteous cry, and the Lord heareth'," she quoted. "That's why I named her Righteous Cry."

"Is your name in the Bible too?" asked Righteous, wiping dirt off her fingers.

"Annie?"

"Naw," giggled Righteous. "Risin' Fawn."

Annie shook her head, looking over to where Charity was hoeing, the crisp sound of the hoe going "chink, chink, chink," as she worked.

"I never thought about where it came from," she said. "My Cherokee name is *Agin'agili*, but nobody calls me that any more."

"I like it," said Righteous, shyly. "I think it's pretty. Tell it to me again so I'll remember."

Chapter Five

Miss Sophia

Annie began her first day at the mission school. She had butterflies in her stomach as she walked up the steps to the one-room log schoolhouse. Because she was starting school after the other children, she had to walk into a room filled with strangers. She tried to tiptoe, but her shoes seemed to make an awful racket on the uneven floor. Students from the primary grades to the higher grades were all in the same room. The youngest children sat at the front of the room and the older students at the back. Annie was given a seat near a window in the middle of the room.

The teacher's desk sat on a high platform at the front of the classroom. A pot-bellied stove in one corner warmed the area around it. Annie later was to learn that the students' parents provided wood for the winter. This supply of wood was called "truck" and helped pay for the cost of school.

Annie kept her eyes down, scarcely looking around the room. No one spoke. Then, a soft voice said *"A siyu,"* and when she heard the Cherokee word for "Hello," Annie felt better almost at once.

The teacher introduced herself as Miss Sophia and Annie was sure that she was the most beautiful lady she'd ever seen. She was slender and her hair was brown and shiny with golden lights. She wore a tiny, gold watch pinned to her white, starched shirtwaist and when she walked, her skirt rustled like leaves. Annie breathed a sigh of relief. Maybe this school thing wouldn't be so awful, after all.

At mid-morning, after Annie had been introduced to the class and had been given her lessons, a visitor entered the classroom. The man was thin and had dark circles under his eyes. He was introduced as the Reverend Worcester. He was in charge of the school and was very nice.

By the end of the day, Annie had been given a copy of the Cherokee syllabary, which was the Cherokee alphabet with oddly-shaped symbols. She already knew that it had been invented by a man named *Sequoya*, a mixed-blood Cherokee. Almost overnight, the Cherokee alphabet made communication possible for all the people. Her mother had taught her to read and write and her father had taught her sums, but she wasn't very good at arithmetic. She ate her lunch that day with the girl who sat behind her whose name was Gordie. Most of the other students were Cherokee, either full-blood, or mixed-blood.

That night, Uncle Williams told her that the Reverend Worcester had just been released from prison. "That's why he looks ill," he said, after Annie told him about meeting Reverend Worcester and how she thought he looked sick.

"He spent two years at hard labor!" said Uncle William.

Annie was shocked. She'd never known anyone who'd been in jail. "What did he do?" she asked. "Did he commit a crime?"

"His only crime was in trying to help our people," said her uncle. "He tried to support us in our fight to keep our lands. The State of Georgia is trying to take them away from us."

"He was arrested for trying to help?" she asked.

"Yes," said Uncle William. "And he was not the only one. But he is a brave, good man and a friend to the Cherokee."

Annie hadn't known that people could go to jail because they were friendly with Indians. More and more, she realized that there was a lot of things she didn't understand. And most of them were worrisome.

Annie and Righteous were sitting in their secret place beneath the great, drooping branches of the oak tree that grew near the banks of the creek. The new place wasn't the same as her beloved sunflower room, but it was still nice. Bees flew back and forth from the sourwood trees at the edge of the meadow to the tangled herbs in Aunt Martha's garden.

It was a bright, November day with the warmth of summer in the sunlight. Ever since Annie had come to her uncle's plantation, she and Righteous had been best friends. She'd never had a best friend before. She felt like she could tell Righteous anything. They'd been talking about *Nanye'hi* and Star Mountain and how much Annie missed it. And even though her uncle and aunt were good to her, she still missed her home and *Nanye'hi*.

"*Nanye'hi* is very brave," she said. "And she's a "Beloved Woman" in the tribe. She can sit in council meetings. There's nothing she can't do."

Righteous shook her head. "Sometimes being brave ain't enough, Annie," she said.

"What do you mean?"

Righteous told Annie about her own father. "And *he*

was brave. He was called *Usman* and he was a great chieftain in his village in Africa.''

"How do you know?" Annie asked, taking off her shoes and stretching out in the soft grass.

" 'Cause I remember," declared Righteous. "He told me when . . . when . . . when we used to be with him. Before . . . .''

"Before what?" asked Annie.

"Before he was sold," whispered Righteous. She looked down, and with a small stick, began drawing in the soft earth.

"Your father was *sold*?" asked Annie, disbelief on her face.

"Uh huh," said Righteous. She looked over at Annie. "We was *all* sold, Annie. How you reckon we got here in the first place?"

For a moment, Annie was so stunned that she couldn't say anything. For some reason, she'd never thought about that. She'd never asked why people from Africa were living as slaves on her uncle's plantation.

"Before Mr. William bought us," said Righteous, "my mama and me lived in another place. I don't exactly know where. I think Savannah. 'Least, that's where Mister William bought us. Somebody else bought my daddy.''

Annie shook her head. "No, Righteous," she said. "That couldn't happen. You can't buy and sell another person. Not another *person*!"

Righteous sighed deeply. "Annie," she said, "sometimes you acts just plain dumb. What you think being slave means? It means somebody owns you!"

Annie had the oddest feeling in the pit of her stomach like when you come upon something awful in the woods, something squirmy. She didn't understand any of it. Could someone sell a person? And why would her own uncle buy a person?

"Why didn't you run away?" she asked. "You could have run away to the woods. You could have hidden someplace. . . ."

"'Cause if you run away, the paterrollers gets you, that's why," said Righteous. "Everybody knows that. They come after you with dogs, mean ol' red-eye dogs."

But Annie persisted. "How could someone sell you? How'd they get you in the first place? Tell me that!"

"I don't know," said Righteous, wrinkling her forehead in an effort to remember. "I don't remember from the beginning. I was only a bitty baby. I know my mama cried a lot but it didn't help. They sold us anyway. Me and my mama and my daddy."

Finally, Annie asked, "Where's your daddy now? What happened to him?"

Righteous shrugged. "I don't know. Mr. William he tried to find him but he was gone. Somebody else done bought him, I 'spect."

Overhead, the sky was robin's egg blue and there was not a cloud to be seen. Off in the fields, workers picked the last of the fall crops, their bodies bending and moving as they worked the rows. It seemed to Annie that the day had dimmed, that a cloud had passed over the sun. Only there were no clouds.

"Come on, Righteous," she said, pulling on her shoes. "I'm tired of this place. Let's go."

Occasionally, Annie would take out her treasures; the beaded moccasins that were now too small, the magic rock, and the coverlet her mama had made for her. As she held them she thought about how life had been on Star Mountain. "I wish the stupid government would leave us alone," she whispered to Rumblegumption who lay on her bed, purring softly. "And I wish the rock was really magic."

The stone gleamed dully in the amber light of the lantern. But no matter how hard she wished, it seemed that nothing could make things right. It seemed like there was not enough magic in the world to help the Cherokees.

Annie was out in the chicken yard feeding the chickens when Uncle William came out to the back fence. He stood there, looking out over the fields. When she finished, she put the old pan back on its hook on the side of the chicken house and went over to him.

"What's the matter, Uncle William?" she asked. "Don't you feel good?" He looked awful, she thought. There were white lines around his mouth and his hand shook slightly as he took hers.

"I've just been told that the government has closed the *Phoenix*, the Cherokee printing press," he said. "They've taken control of the paper and forbidden its printing of the news."

Annie wasn't sure just how bad that was but from the way Uncle William looked, it must be bad. "What does that mean?" she asked.

"It means we won't be able to print the news of what's happening in the Nation," he said. "We have lost our freedom of the press."

She knew about the paper. Miss Sophie had brought copies for the class to read. *The Phoenix*, which was the name of the paper, was printed in both Cherokee and English. Mr. Boudinot, who was the editor, was a Cherokee. The press was also the place where their schoolbooks were printed.

"Will somebody else print our books?" she asked.

"No, Annie," said Uncle William. "And I'm afraid it's only a matter of time until the school is closed, too. We aren't going to be allowed to educate our children."

The newspaper was soon closed as was the printing press. But the people of the Nation were not silenced. One night, for the first time in her life, Annie heard the drums, the ancient way of sending messages. It was a way of communicating that couldn't be stilled by the government. She stood out in the front yard and way off in the distance, heard a drum beating. It was echoed by another drum, then another, until all over the hills and valleys the people heard the news.

Annie listened and felt the beat of the drums pulsing through her body like her own heartbeat. The drums signalled the end of the Cherokee Nation.

Chapter Six

Head of Coosa

Annie closed her eyes, loving the way the wind blew against her face. The horses seemed to fly over the road, the tiny silver bells attached to their manes ringing in the cold, crisp air. She and her aunt and uncle were on their way to visit John Ross, the chief of the Cherokee Nation. The trip to "Head of Coosa," which was the name of the chief's house, was half a day's drive from the Blackfeather plantation.

They entered the drive leading up to the chief's house and Annie saw for the first time the white house that was surrounded by gardens that in summer were filled with roses. When she was introduced to Chief Ross and his wife, Quatie, Annie could hardly keep from staring. Mrs. Ross was beautiful. She wore a gown of silvery silk that was the color of a mountain stream and her voice held laughter in it. The chief was short and stocky and very kind. Uncle William had told her that Chief Ross was a mixed-blood who chose to live as Cherokee.

While the grownups talked, Annie was allowed to go for a walk in the garden. Because it was winter, there were no roses blooming but the garden was filled with color. Red-birds darted in and out of thorny shrubs, eating the bright orange berries. Scuppernong vines were golden and held the grapes whose skins were speckled with bronze spots.

As she stood looking at the grapes, Annie heard a violent shriek behind her. She jumped and turned quickly, her heart pounding. There, directly behind her was a strange, glossy bird with a blue neck. He trailed a long train of feathers and as she watched, he raised the tail of his feathers into a shimmering fan, each brilliant blue feather centered with a golden eye. Annie was rooted to the spot.

As she stood there, Chief Ross joined her. He wasn't nearly as tall as Uncle William but his shoulders were broad and strong under his blue waistcoat.

"It's a peacock," he said, smiling at her surprise. Reaching down, he picked up a fallen feather. "Our people call these 'star-feathers'," he told her. Then he told her the Cherokee legend of stars being creatures with feathers.

When she left to go home, the chief gave Annie a sheath of brilliant peacock feathers. He and Mrs. Ross seemed happy as they waved goodbye from the veranda. But the next time she saw the chief, he would be a hunted man and his beautiful home would have been taken over by strangers. The chief and his wife would be homeless in their own land.

More and more soldiers appeared in town. There was a rumor that the school would soon be closed and the teachers arrested, but only a few people believed it. Those who did however, took their children out of school and the class grew smaller and smaller each week.

There was a terrible ice storm the week before Christmas. Annie awoke during the night and heard the tops of the pine trees popping like firecrackers. In the morning, the world looked like a fairyland. Ice crystals shimmered like diamonds on each branch of each tree and hung from the eaves of the house like shining jewels.

On Christmas Eve, Annie and Righteous bundled up in shawls and caps and mittens. Uncle William was going to the woods to cut the Christmas tree and they were going with him. Annie had never had a Christmas tree before. In the mountains, her father had cut fragrant boughs of balsam, but they didn't decorate a tree.

The grass crackled underfoot and the air was sweet with the scent of pine. They searched until they found the perfect tree. It was a tall cedar with dark, feathery branches. Uncle William put it into the back of the wagon. Annie could hardly wait to get back to decorate it with the strands of berries she and Righteous had strung. Then, tiny white candles would be attached to the branches.

On Christmas morning, Annie was given a new dress of soft, rose-colored wool and both she and Righteous received new boots, especially cut from deerskin. Annie was surprised because the boots were Indian boots and Aunt Martha hadn't wanted her to wear Indian dress. But lately, Aunt Martha seemed different in a lot of ways. It was as though she had begun to like Cherokee ways and customs better than she had in the past.

On a cool, spring night, Annie was sitting in the parlour struggling with a bit of embroidery that her aunt had begun for her. "Every young girl should make a sampler," she'd said. Annie's was a square of linen with the alphabet to be worked in cross-stitch and a verse that was supposed to be four lines that read:

AND YOU EACH GENTLE ANIMAL
IN CONFIDENCE MAY BIND,

AND MAKE THEM FOLLOW AT YOUR CALL,
IF YOU ARE ALWAYS KIND.

The verse was from a poem by a lady named Sarah
Josepha Hale. Annie's lines looked more like hen
scratching than letters.

Jabbing the needle through the cloth, Annie made a
triple knot and wadded the sampler into a ball. Just as
she started to cut the thread, Charity came into the room.

"There's a message from Chief Ross," she said, handing an envelope to Uncle William.

Annie finally bit off the thread and looked up, aware
that the room had grown very quiet. The crackle of the
fire was the only sound in the room. Uncle William
finished reading the letter and passed it to Aunt Martha.

"That's that, then," he said, rising and going over to
the fire where he stood gazing into the flames.

"What's the matter?" asked Annie, suddenly frightened by the way her uncle looked.

"The State has taken over everything that Chief Ross
owns," said Uncle William. His voice was muffled and
strange. "The chief has gone to Tennessee for safety. He
managed to save only a few of his papers."

"They've taken everything?" asked Annie. "His house
and horses? Even the peacocks?"

"Everything," said Uncle William.

Aunt Martha hadn't made a sound. She just sat, looking down at the letter in her hands. Goosebumps popped
up on Annie's arms. Chief Ross was the most powerful
man in the entire Nation. If *his* home could be taken, if
he could be threatened, what would happen to the rest
of the Cherokee people?

She recalled *Nanye'hi*'s words that last night on Star
Mountain. "A great and fierce wind will sweep over the

lands of the Cherokee, killing and scattering our people like leaves." Was this what *Nanye'hi* had meant? The words had drifted in and out of her sleep that night, but now she remembered. Was this the rising of the wind?

One morning, Miss Sophia came into the classroom and stood in front of the class. She was pale and looked unhappy. There was a hush in the room.

"I have an announcement to make," she said. She cleared her throat. Her eyes were bright with unshed tears. "This will be my last day here with you," she said softly. "I am leaving the Cherokee Nation."

For a moment, there was a silence in the room as though someone had put a cover over it. No one spoke. A book dropped at the back of the room and someone coughed. Then, everyone began talking at once. Miss Sophia held up her hand for silence.

"I have been given a new assignment," she said. "You all know how much I hate to leave. I have loved the Nation and I have loved you. This will be a hard thing for all of us. We must pray for the Nation." Her voice broke slightly and she looked away. "I wish I could tell you more, but I don't understand what is happening either. The missionaries are being sent to a new school and we will all leave soon. If God is willing, I will return to the Cherokee Nation. And soon, I hope, soon."

Annie wondered if she would ever see Miss Sophia again. And she wondered too, why Miss Sophia, who was not Indian, could be forced to leave the place and the people she loved.

After Miss Sophia left, Annie began to hate school. Most of the Indian students were leaving and the new students were unfriendly and unkind. They were whites whose parents had been given Indian lands. They acted as though they, and not the Cherokee, belonged.

But Miss Sophia would not give up teaching the Cherokee children. She was offered space at Running Waters, the home of Major John Ridge, a man called "The Ridge," by the Cherokees. The Ridge had fought with Andrew Jackson at the Battle of Horseshoe Bend. He offered Miss Sophia a place to live and a classroom for her pupils. But because of Uncle William's disagreement with The Ridge's politics, Annie was not allowed to attend Miss Sophia's school.

School ended for Annie. Aunt Martha began tutoring her at home. With Miss Sophia gone, Annie didn't mind being out of school. For the rest of the school year and into the next fall, Annie and Righteous were taught together.

On a day in late September, Annie came in from the meadow, where she'd been watching as the bees flew in and out of the bee skeps, making what Uncle William called "a bee line" from the sourwood trees. As she went into the kitchen, she overheard her aunt telling Charity, "It's getting harder and harder to make life seem normal." But things weren't normal. Nothing was right. Uncle William was so tired that his eyes were red-rimmed and his hands shook slightly. Men came and went at the house all during the day and sometimes late at night. Annie was often awakened by the sound of hoofbeats on the drive outside her window. There were secret meetings in Uncle William's study and most nights, when she went to bed, she heard the low murmur of voices until she fell asleep.

Chapter Seven

The Ridge Group

Frost glittered like sugar crystals on fences and in the fields. Woodsmoke rose in straight columns into the sky and the sound of carriage bells rang sweetly in the cold air. There was a feeling of excitement in town, much like the excitement of a fair or festival. Everyone had gathered in the town square.

"There may be six hundred people here," said Uncle William from where he stood on the steps of the Council House.

The first group of Cherokees leaving for the West had assembled, awaiting the signal to leave. They were called "the Ridge Group," because they were being led into the new territory by Major Ridge, who was one of the Cherokee leaders.

There were women wearing furs, sitting in carriages. Men on horseback wore feathers braided into their hair and children laughed and waved from where they were sitting next to their mothers in the carriages. Annie and Righteous waved to them and one little girl blew Annie a kiss.

The State of Georgia had announced its plans to take over Indian lands and the federal government had said that the Indians would be wise to plan to move to the west to establish a *new* Cherokee Nation. Some of the people had decided that since they would soon have to leave their lands anyway, they might as well be paid for them. Even though the price offered wasn't fair, it was better than nothing, some said. They also wanted to be able to leave without troops to guide them as had been threatened.

Surprisingly, there were no soldiers in town, or at least, not in the square that morning. A man slipped through the crowd and joined Uncle William on the steps.

"Chief Ross!" exclaimed Uncle William, when he saw who it was. "I didn't think you'd make it."

"I had to," said the chief. "I had to see my people on their way."

Chief Ross had been in hiding from the authorities since his house was taken over by armed troops. He explained that he'd come down from Tennessee where he'd been given safe lodging, in order to see the Ridge Group leave for the new territory. He watched sadly as some of the people called out to him. Shaking his head, he said, "I will never leave this land voluntarily. Never!"

"Nor I," said Uncle William. "Not while there is breath in my body. This is my land and I won't give it up."

After the Ridge Group left, things sort of settled down for awhile. The government and the State of Georgia seemed to back away. Perhaps because so many people had left, but no one was quite sure. No one was quite sure of anything.

Finally, the long winter ended. It seemed to Annie that overnight the branches of the trees were filled with tiny, green buds. In the woods, catkins of pussywillows gleamed soft and silvery and there were bluebirds nesting in the fence posts. Dogwood trees bloomed pink in the woods and the outlines of the hills were visible through tender spring growth.

Annie was allowed to take off her thick, woolen stockings and exchange them for lighter ones of cotton. Her winter clothes were laid away in a trunk and covered with camphor. Aunt Martha and Charity began the annual spring cleaning. But Uncle William held off the planting of new crops although his neighbors began working in the fields in March.

In Washington, Chief Ross approached President Van Buren as he had approached President Andrew Jackson, to plead for the Cherokees. But while Van Buren was not as insensitive as Jackson had been, it was to no avail. Governor Gilmer in Georgia was insisting that if the Cherokees did not leave, he would send in the militia to move them. He wanted the Indian lands and he wanted them now.

Chapter Eight

Building Stockades

The silvery, weathered boards of the grist mill blended with the trunks of the oak trees that surrounded it, so that it looked as though it had grown there by the swiftly running stream. Wild cress and mint grew along the banks where the huge granite wheel turned, scattering silver drops of water into the sunlight.

Annie and Righteous sat in the wagon waiting for Uncle William. He had gone inside to have corn freshly ground and to pay the miller for the grinding. Horseflies buzzed around the rumps of the horses and the sun was directly overhead.

"It's too hot to sit in this old wagon," said Annie, fanning herself with her skirt. "I'm gettin' down from here." She slid along the seat and jumped to the ground.

"I don't think we ought to," said Righteous, looking over her shoulder at the mill where the shutters were closed against the heat of the sun.

"Why not?" asked Annie. "Come on, Righteous. We'll go wait in the shade." In the heat, Annie's hair curled softly at her temples. She sat on the bank and rolled her stockings down around her ankles.

Righteous followed Annie over to the banks of the creek. The water was clear and rippled into eddies and tiny whirlpools. The air smelled of mint and fresh growing things.

Annie looked over at Righteous. "How come you're acting so funny?" she asked.

"I ain't acting funny," said Righteous.

"Yes, you are," said Annie. "And you keep looking around all the time."

Righteous moved closer to Annie. "Annie," she whispered, "I declare. Sometimes you act like . . . well, I don't know. Seem like you in a dream. You don't know nothin'!"

"I do too," said Annie. "Like what?"

"Like your uncle ain't jest gettin' corn ground in the mill," she said. "They's a secret meetin' goin' on. I heard Mister William tellin' Miss Martha. 'Martha', he say. 'It's all right to take them with me.'"

"You mean us?" said Annie.

"Yes. And Miss Martha, she say, 'It be's dangerous. I be's worriet about them.' But he say, 'No one's gonna' bother them. They safe with me'."

"I don't believe it!" said Annie, excitedly. "What kind of meeting?"

Just then, they heard horses coming along the trail leading to the mill. Two horsemen approached and tying their horses to the pitching post, walked quickly inside the mill.

Righteous pinched Annie hard on the arm. "See!" she said. "That's Mister Will Thomas and . . . and . . . ."

"And Chief Ross!" said Annie.

"Lordy," said Righteous. "And in broad daylight. C'mon, Annie. Let's move closer to the mill. Just in case."

The hairs rose on the back of Annie's neck. "Suppose the soldiers come!"

It was getting harder and harder for Cherokees to meet for any reason. Public meetings were not allowed. The newspaper was closed and the only way the people could get the news was from secret meetings. The mill was one place where two or more people could meet without causing suspicion.

The water wheel creaked gently in the heat of the afternoon. Annie and Righteous lay on their stomachs in the soft grass. "Righteous," said Annie, "I'm really worried about Aunt Martha. I think she's sick."

"How come?" asked Righteous.

"Well," said Annie. "She just acts sick, kind of. Like she's tired or disappointed all the time. And she prays a lot, too."

"So does my mama," said Righteous. "I reckon it's 'cause the government is gonna' take away her house. I 'spec Miss Martha is scared about that. She owns that big old house and the barn and the cabins. I wouldn't like it if somebody took *my* home away."

"They will," said Annie.

"Oh, yeah," said Righteous. "I forgot for a minute."

A few minutes later, Uncle William came out of the mill. He climbed back in the wagon and the girls joined him. He didn't say a single word all the way home.

That night, after supper, Righteous and Annie sat on the front porch. Lamplight spilled onto the porch in golden squares and they could see Charity's shadow as she passed back and forth from the dining room. The whirring of katydids rose and fell.

"Why don't we fight?" asked Annie. "We could dig a moat. Keep the soldiers out."

"They's too many of 'em," said Righteous. "We couldn't win."

"How about if we all ran away to Star Mountain?" Annie asked. "They'd never find us there." She picked up a small stone from the ground near the steps. "Would that be cowardly if we ran away?"

"I don't think so," said Righteous. "It don't make no sense jest to sit here and wait to be locked up."

"I'll talk to Uncle William," said Annie. "Maybe he's got a secret plan we don't know about."

"I sho' hope so," said Righteous, pulling her dress down tightly over her knees and looking out at the darkened garden.

"Maybe we could build a fort like the one on the river," said Annie.

"Wouldn't do no good," said Righteous.

"You reckon they're really gonna' put us in those stockades?" asked Annie.

Righteous shrugged her shoulders. Out in the garden, lightning bugs flickered greeny gold. Honeysuckle smelled sweet and lemony.

"I don't see how they can make us do that," said Annie. "We haven't done anything wrong. It isn't fair!"

"I think we ought to run away," said Righteous. " 'Cept I'm scared of patterrollers."

"I think they'd send the soldiers after us," said Annie. "And they have guns."

"Soldiers always have guns," said Righteous gloomily.

In the study, Charity stood in front of Uncle William's desk. She looked at the paper in her hand, then back at Uncle William. The lamplight shone on his face, showing lines of grief and sadness that had not been there a year ago. Charity couldn't read so she asked, "Mr. William, does this paper say that I'm free in the eyes of the law?"

"Yes," he replied. "That's what it says. I have freed all

my slaves. No one owns you or Righteous. No one may ever call you "slave" again. You and your child are free now." He looked down at his desk. "Now that it may be too late," he said softly. "Charity, I hope you will forgive me. I should have known, but I didn't. Until I felt the anger at the loss of my own freedom, I didn't realize how much I had taken from you and the others. Now I know just how precious freedom is. I hope you can find it in your heart to forgive me."

"Mister William," said Charity, "I do thank you. I do. But you see, I was always free. In my heart, I was free. But I thanks you for your kindness. And for making things better for my child." She carefully folded the paper, smoothing it with her long fingers. "We don't have to wait here for the soldiers to come get us. We can run away, Mr. William. Lots of folks have run away to the mountains. We could do that. We'd be like the little foxes, we'd hide 'til all this is over."

The room had darkened as twilight deepened. Uncle William touched a match to the candle on his desk. It bloomed in the dusk, casting a golden light.

"No, Charity," he said. "I must go with my people. Those of us who survive the journey will be needed to help rebuild a new Nation. There will be children who will lose their parents on the trail. They'll need Martha and me. Perhaps we'll be able to start a new life. Build a new home. Some of our people are already there. And maybe, just maybe, Martha and I will find something out there. But there is no need for you and Righteous to go. One crime needn't lead to another. You all were brought here against your will. That was *my* doing. This was never your home. Now, you can make a new life. It won't be easy, but at least you won't be locked up in the stockade. I'll see to that!"

He turned to the window and looked out over the fields. Mists had begun to fill the hollows and valleys, wreathing the trees in silver veils.

"Oh, but I will miss this land, Charity," he said softly. "This land is my heart. I will grieve forever for this place."

Then, from the center drawer of the desk, he withdrew a small, leather sack.

"This is only a small part of what I owe you," he said, handing it to Charity. "Take it. It is half of what I own now. I'm putting it in your care. Make a new life for Annie and Righteous."

Charity stood straight and tall. "Don't you fret, Mister William. Those chirren will be jest fine. They got me to see to it. And, Mr. William. . . ."

"Yes, Charity?"

"God bless you. And Miss Martha."

After Charity had gone, Uncle William blew out the candle on the desk and went over to the window. He watched the first stars bloom against the night sky. The moon rose like a golden pumpkin, shining on the place where his heart dwelled and he could not.

The household was awakened early one morning when a rider came up the drive with an urgent message for Uncle William. Minutes later, Uncle William rode down the drive as though something were after him. The horse's hoofs scattered pebbles as he raced away.

"What do you suppose it's about?" Annie asked her aunt at breakfast. She had seen her uncle race down the drive earlier.

Aunt Martha shook her head. "It's bad news," she said. "I can just feel it."

The notice had been posted on the Council House

door. All hope was lost. Governor Gilmer, from the capital at Milledgeville, had announced that the whites had the right to move onto Indian lands. The Cherokees would be forced to move. And the governor was being backed by the U.S. Government. Federal troops were on their way to New Echota.

When he returned from town, Uncle William called his household together. The word was out. General Winfield Scott was on his way to New Echota. He would headquarter at the Council House, using it as barracks for his troops. There were seven thousand U.S. regulars and volunteers under his command. And if this force were not enough, he could call on the governors of adjoining states for four thousand more troops.

Uncle William stood next to the window in the study.

"The government has started building stockades here, in New Echota."

"What?" said Aunt Martha, her eyes wide with horror. "I never believed that! They can't!"

"They can and they are," said Uncle William. "They are building prisons for Indians. For us. The state is taking over everything—our homes, our farms, our livestock. And when everything is gone, they plan to put us, and members of our households, into stockades. To round us up like cattle and then move us west."

"But William," said Aunt Martha. "John Ross went to Washington to plead for us. There were newspaper articles! Daniel Webster spoke for us! How can this happen?"

"It's too late, my dear," said Uncle William, taking Aunt Martha's hands. "It's too late. We are betrayed."

Charity threw her apron up over her head. "Oh, sweet Lord," she cried. "Oh, my sweet Lord!"

Righteous reached for Annie's hand. Neither of them

said a word. They were too scared. If the grownups were this worried, things were really bad. Annie had never been so frightened in her life. What would happen now? And how much time did they have before the soldiers came for them?

Gradually, word began to arrive from those Cherokees who had gone ahead with the Ridge Party to Arkansas. There had been much sickness along the way and some had died. But the people were homesick, too. What they found wasn't what they'd hoped for but it was too late. They had to make the best of what was there for them.

All over the country, people protested the treatment of the Indians, but it did no good. The government had ordered the Indians out of Georgia. And they had to go. A young poet and philosopher, unknown at the time, Ralph Waldo Emerson, wrote a letter to the President: " . . . the mercy that is that heart's heart in all men, from Maine to Georgia, does abhor this business. . . ."

Chapter Nine

The Beginning of the Trail

Yellow roses twined around the posts on the front porch and tumbled over the railings. Cupping one of the blossoms in her hand, Annie closed her eyes and took a deep breath.

"It smells like tea," she said blissfully, "and something else . . . something. . . . "

"Like heaven," said Righteous.

It was mid-afternoon and the day was so hot that down in the pond, cows stood rump-deep in the water. The cotton was high in the fields but there were no workers to pick it. The fields stretched out green and silent, the cotton bolls dotting the green like bits of snow.

Rumblegumption lay stretched out on her back, her front and back paws in the air, occasionally turning on her side as she lost her balance. Summer butterflies hovered over the mint bed but she ignored them. It was too hot to chase butterflies. She closed her eyes and stretched, allowing Righteous to scratch her stomach.

"Let's go wade," said Annie, getting up from the steps. "I'm hot." She and Righteous were barefoot. Aunt Martha no longer insisted that Annie wear stockings.

She stepped out onto the front yard and stood in the grass. Suddenly, she turned to Righteous.

"Something's happening!" she said. "I can feel it!" Through the soles of her feet she felt something moving, something big. The vibrations made her scalp prickle. "Hurry up!" she said to Righteous. "Come feel!"

Righteous went out into the yard and she too, felt the movement of the earth beneath her feet. She pointed toward the horizon, past the fields that shimmered in the heat.

"Something's on fire!"

A cloud hung low on the horizon. It was grey and red and moved slowly in the afternoon heat. "You reckon the town's on fire?" Annie asked, a sense of dread coming over her.

"I don't know," said Righteous, "but I'm gonna' go get my mama. You wait for me!"

All afternoon, the people rode past the plantation. They came on foot, on mules, some in wagons. Children walked with their mothers, a few held kittens or puppies in their arms. Old people sat in the backs of wagons, their heads down, their shoulders hunched. No one spoke. Only the creaking of the wagons and the horses' hoofs sounded on the warm air. The Cherokees were being led to the stockades before making the long trail west.

Holding on to the fencepost, Annie watched as the people passed by. She felt a tug on her skirt.

"Get back here," hissed Righteous, pulling her back into the shelter of plum trees that grew near the fence.

"They'll get us too!"

At some point, Aunt Martha and Charity had come outside and set up a table on which sat a bucket of cool water and dried gourds for drinking. Next to the bucket were baskets of apples—the first of the season—which they were offering to the people as they passed.

Clouds of dust filled the air, making their throats dry

and raw. The air was thick. A young soldier rode over to where Aunt Martha was filling gourds with water.

"Ma'am," he said, taking off his cap. "Could I have some water?"

For a moment, it looked as though Aunt Martha were going to refuse but then the soldier said, "It's for her," pointing over his shoulder to where an old woman lay in a wagon. Filling the gourd, Aunt Martha handed it to him and when he returned, he dismounted and again, taking off his cap, thanked her. His hair, where it was not powdered with dust, was blonde. "We're under orders, Ma'am," he said. "This is not the kind of work I signed up to do."

"What's your name?" Aunt Martha asked, handing him an apple.

"Burnett, Ma'am. Private John G. Burnett. Second Regiment Mounted Infantry."

"You look awfully young," said Aunt Martha. "How old are you?"

"I'm sixteen, Ma'am."

"Does your mama know what kind of work you're doing?" she asked.

"My mama's passed away," said the young soldier. "I don't have any folks. The army's my family now."

"Well, it's not doing right by you," snapped Aunt Martha. "This is sorry work indeed."

"Yes'm," he said. "It grieves me to do it."

"I'll pray for you," said Aunt Martha. "And for all of us."

Annie didn't know she was crying until she tasted the salt of her tears on her lips. At the end of the first day, they were all tired, dirty, and heartsick. The four of them walked slowly back up to the house, wondering if the next day would bring more suffering and pain.

The stockades were built on the outskirts of New Echota. They were like camps but with high walls made of logs with the ends sharpened. The Cherokees would remain prisoners until it was time for the long journey west. Then, the people would walk and ride, mile after lonely mile, all the way from Georgia to the Arkansas. Some were put on steamers and transported down the Tennessee and Ohio Rivers to the farther side of the Mississippi, where they continued their journey by land to the west. Most however, went overland, crossing to the north side of the Hiwassee at a ferry, they proceeded down the river. The old, the sick and the smaller children in wagons, the rest on foot or on horses.

Long lines of people passed in front of the plantation for days. And each day, Aunt Martha, Charity, Annie, and Righteous offered cool water and apples. It was not much but it was what they could do. During those days, Aunt Martha wore a cloth wrapped around her head and an apron that covered her from neck to ankles. It was the first time that Annie had seen her aunt when she didn't look perfectly dressed.

At the end of each day, Aunt Martha's hair hung lankly from the bun at the back of her head. Her dress was filthy as was her apron and there were thin lines down her face where her tears had made tracks through the dust.

Finally, the people stopped coming by and the road was deserted except for an occasional scouting party or a few soldiers on foot. For some reason, Uncle William's family and household were not bothered. Perhaps because John Ross had told General Scott that Uncle William was a man of his word and could be trusted not to try to escape. And too, Uncle William had already said that he planned to make the trip to the west.

Plans were made for the final departure of the Cherokees. Now, except for a few families near New Echota and some at Ross's Landing, nearly all the Indians were in stockades. There were nearly 16,000 men, women, and children and members of Indian households being held prisoner in Georgia.

Then, just when things looked darkest for the Cherokees, there was a ray of hope. John Ross was allowed to visit the camps and to make a report of the conditions to General Scott. Ross proposed that in the fall the Cherokees be allowed to make the journey on their own. They would be on the honor system to go, but without military escort. Surprisingly, this request was granted. It was a thing that had not been allowed to the Creeks, Chickasaws, or Seminoles. At this time, too, Ross saw to it that conditions at the camps improved.

The government was no longer calling the Indians, "prisoners." However, since their homes had been taken away, that is what they were. Ross and other Cherokee leaders formed a committee to try to get some payment back for the land and houses taken from them. The people were allowed to submit bills to the government. Wealthy Cherokees billed the government for fine houses, silverware, blooded horses, and fine libraries. And poor people sent in bills, as one woman did for the loss of "six ducks, a plaid cloak, a feather bed, a turkey gobbler, a set of china, two blowguns, a fiddle, garden tools, an umbrella, a coffee pot and a plow."

Since Ross had taken over the overseeing of the camps, the people were not so sad. General Scott cooperated with the chief in collecting equipment for the journey.

There would be 645 wagons, five thousand horses, and several boats for river transportation for the ill and old. But no sooner were promises made than they were broken. The government turned a blind eye towards the Cherokees. The Reverend Evan Jones, a Baptist preacher who visited the stockades, said that the Cherokees were "prisoners, without a crime to justify the fact." Then, another promise was broken. The people would *not* be allowed to travel west on their own, but would be herded like cattle by troops.

They were supposed to leave in late September, but a summer drought wasted the land. There was not enough food or water for the animals to make the move. Chief Ross asked for more time. October 1st was set as the final deadline.

Meanwhile, at the Blackfeather plantation, plans were being made for another kind of move, one that directly concerned Annie and Righteous.

Chapter Ten

The Plan

The crackling fire threw long shadows against the rough walls of Charity's cabin. The shutters were closed against the night and the room smelled of woodsmoke and drying herbs. In the firelight, Charity's face was grave as she listened while Uncle William explained the plan to her.

"There is one thing in our favor," he said. "Annie has never been listed as a permanent member of this household. I've been very careful *not* to list her. And you and Righteous are now free blacks. There is no earthly reason why you all should suffer the fate of the Cherokees."

From where she sat near the fire, Annie listened carefully. Something was wrong about all this, she thought. Why should she be allowed to go free when Uncle William and Aunt Martha faced the trail with the others?

"I can't!" she blurted out suddenly. "It's not fair!"

Uncle William turned to her. "We've talked about 'fair' before, Annie," he said. "Fair has nothing to do with it. We have to deal with what is. There are enough people at risk already. You needn't be. I brought you here from your home. Now, I'm going to help you go back."

"But . . . " she began.

"No, Annie," he said firmly. "It's settled. You and Righteous will make a run for it. Soon, Charity will follow. We've made arrangements with a nice family who will help her when the time comes. It will be easier if you and Righteous go first. The three of you traveling together would be too suspicious. This is all a risk. But you're brave. And you're a child of the mountains, *Agin'agili*. You need to go home now.''

"But it's running away!" she said.

"No!" said Uncle William fiercely. "It's running *to*. It's not the same thing."

"You won't think I'm turning my back on you?" she asked.

"No, my dear. You will be facing the mountain. Star Mountain is your home." He came over and took her hands in his. "It will make me happy to know that at least a part of me will be here in the land of our people. You will be that part of me."

"Why isn't Charity going with us?" Annie asked.

"I've told you," he said. "She'll come later."

"I'm gonna' stay here for a little while," said Charity. "I need to help Miss Martha. When she's better, and not feeling so bad about everything, I'll come to you all."

"But what if you can't find us?" wailed Righteous, speaking for the first time that night. "What if you lose us?"

Charity took Righteous into her arms. "I won't lose you, chile," she said. "No matter what, no matter where you are, I'll find you. This ol' earth ain't big enough to hide you from me."

Annie turned to Righteous. "We'll find our way home," she said, with more conviction than she felt. "Don't you worry. We'll get back to Star Mountain and *Nanye'hi*, and Charity will come too."

The plan was for the girls to leave before dawn on a certain day. They would ride the back paths and little-known trails up to the mountains. There Will Thomas, whose Cherokee name was *Wil-Usdi*, or "Little Will," would meet them and take them to his mother who lived with him at Qualla, on the banks of the Oconaluftee River. Little Will, who was white, had been adopted by Chief *Yonaguska* (Drowning Bear), after the death of Will's father. He had learned the Cherokee language and when he grew up, he moved with his mother to Qualla. He owned five trading stores and was one of the best friends the Cherokees had. As a lawyer, he was able to help them with their legal problems, like buying land and owning gold, both of which were forbidden by law now.

At his store, Annie and Righteous would get the supplies they would need for the winter on Star Mountain. Then he would escort them most of the way up the mountain to where they'd be safe.

"The first part of the journey you'll have to make alone," said Uncle William. "Little Will has other obligations. There aren't enough people to help those trying to escape. But he'll meet you and you'll be safe with him. He has property in the North Carolina mountains and he's acting as agent for the Cherokees who have managed to escape to the hills. Because he's white, he can buy property. He buys it in his name, but it belongs to the Indians. He's a good man and a good friend."

"Will we get to meet his father, Chief *Yonaguska*?" asked Annie.

"I imagine so," said Uncle William. "His home is right across the river from Will's place." He explained that Chief *Yonaguska* was a powerful chief. That he was a peace chief and counselor. "He is a powerful speaker," said Uncle William.

A cold wind blew out of the hills, chilling the land

and bringing color to the trees. The days grew shorter and the nights longer. Fires burned in the fireplaces and nearly every night Uncle William and Aunt Martha talked long into the night.

There was a feeling of sadness over the land that was so strong Annie felt she could reach out and touch it. The very air seemed heavy with despair and unhappiness. Everyone was hoping for a miracle that would save the Cherokees; a miracle that would allow the people to remain in their own land. And the land was especially beautiful that year. Perhaps it seemed more beautiful because it was the last autumn the people would see in Georgia. But time moved on and grew short.

Aunt Martha began packing the supplies the girls would need for the journey. There were hard-baked breads, dried venison and beef, honey, sunflower seeds, and dried fruits. She showed them how to soak the fruit overnight so that it would be plump and good. When Annie saw the sunflower seeds she remembered her own sunflower room. "God's gold," her father had called the flowers that followed the sun.

"We can't pack too much," said Charity, "because you have to travel light. But it will last you 'til you gets to Qualla."

Charity wrapped cornmeal in cloth bags that had been coated with wax to keep out moisture. She packed tin cups, a sharp knife, a small frying pan, a box of matches called "Lucifers," and a few sweet potatoes that they could bake in the campfire. "You don't want to take too much," she said, and as soon as the words were out of her mouth, her eyes got teary and she went quickly out of the room.

They were waiting for the rains. Uncle William had said that when the rains came, there would be so much going on in preparation for the Cherokees' journey that the girls could slip away unnoticed. Day after day, an entire people waited and watched for rain.

Then, late one night, Annie heard a light pattering on the roof. From the distance, came the low growl of thunder. It had begun. The rains began softly, the great heavy drops making rings in the dry, dusty earth. It rained harder and the wind blew, banging the shutters against the house and waking the members of the household. Streams filled and swelled and ponds grew deeper. Trees loomed black against the sky and tree frogs sang all night long. The air freshened and smelled sweet.

Annie lay in her bed listening to the rain. She thought about how far Star Mountain was and how lonely and long the path leading back. Pulling the coverlet over her head, she was grateful for the warmth of Rumblegumption, who lay stretched along her back.

Aunt Martha stood behind Annie as she sat in front of the looking glass. "We have to change your appearance," she said, as she cut Annie's hair. "You will look less like a Cherokee with your hair cut short. And it will grow back. What's important now is that you attract as little attention as possible. If anyone sees you, you want them to think you're a Scot, like your father."

Annie ran her fingers through her short, cropped hair and thought, No, they won't think I'm a Cherokee girl. They'll think I'm a Cherokee boy. Still, anything to help them escape.

The rains stopped. Uncle William locked himself in his study going over the map he'd drawn up for them with Mr. Will's help. Aunt Martha packed and re-packed Annie's things. Finally, she went to her room, returning with a small Bible that she placed on top of Annie's coverlet.

"It was mine when I was a girl," she said. "I want you to have it."

Righteous said a tearful farewell to Joshua. Annie looked for Rumblegumption, but in the mysterious way of cats, she'd disappeared, upset and knowing that something was wrong. It's all too hard, Annie thought, fighting back tears. Nothing's supposed to be this hard.

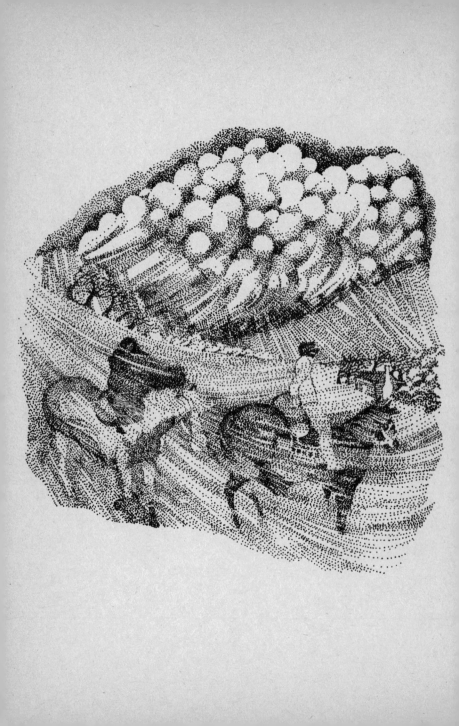

Chapter Eleven

A Cabin in the Woods

The stars were still blooming in the early morning sky when Aunt Martha came to awaken Annie. She stood in the doorway, a lamp held high, its light spilling gold over her black dress.

"It's time, Annie," she said softly.

Annie felt as though she'd been awake forever. She mumbled sleepily, "It can't be. I just got to sleep."

"Still," said Aunt Martha. "We have to hurry before first light."

Finally, everything was in readiness. Aunt Martha and Uncle William stood together at the bottom of the steps. Aunt Martha was pale in the light from the lantern, but she was calm as she took Annie into her arms. Smoothing back Annie's newly cropped hair, she whispered, "Go with God, Annie." Then, her mouth went crooked and she blinked back tears.

Charity held both girls to her ample bosom. "I'll be there soon," she said. "Don't you worry." Righteous clung to her mother, then stepped back. She was wearing a dark shawl that covered her from head to hem. Suspended on a cord around her neck, was the bag of coins that would pay for the supplies they'd have to buy at Qualla. The coins were heavy and from time to time, she'd reach up and touch the bag to make sure it was still there. She looked over at Annie as Uncle William brought the horses around to the front.

"I think I'm gonna' throw up," she whispered.

"No, you aren't," Annie whispered back. "If you do, I will, too, and I hate it."

Then Annie threw her father's old tartan over the saddle. In her pack, she had the maps and the magic rock. Now that she was going home, maybe she would find out just what the magic rock was for and why it was magic. *If* it was magic, she thought.

Uncle William took Annie in his arms. "It's good that you're returning to Star Mountain and *Nanye'hi*. Be strong and true to your heritage. It's a proud one."

Annie's heart was beating like a bird in her breast. She could barely breathe. Then, as Uncle William held the stirrups for her, she mounted her horse. Turning then, Uncle William picked up a slender stalk of the yellow rose that in summer tumbled in silken bells over the front porch. Bare now, its roots were carefully wrapped in burlap.

"Plant this by the cabin door," he said, "and in spring when the roses bloom, remember us."

At the edge of the lawn, Annie turned and looked back. The big old house was dark except for the lantern on the porch. She waved goodbye and as she did, heard Righteous hiccup, trying to keep back her tears.

The girls rode into the woods where the dew was silvery and where mists hung low in the trees. Pine trees glistened with silver drops that fell as they rode beneath the branches.

Uncle William had gone over the map with them very carefully, marking their way. They planned to stay off the main roads, riding through fields and woods and along little-known Indian paths.

At dusk on the first night, they stopped at a natural clearing in the woods. Annie watered the horses while Righteous gathered firewood. As she looked around, Annie felt that the woods were closing in. It was the time of day that she dreaded most, when everything seems distant and lonely. She wondered if Righteous felt the same way.

They placed their blankets by the fire and ate their supper of bread and honey and cheese.

"Well," said Righteous, licking honey off her fingers, "we got this far."

"Yep," said Annie, "we sure did."

"Guess we ought to go to sleep," said Righteous, looking over her shoulder at the dark woods behind them.

"I reckon," said Annie. She was so tired she could hardly move but she was afraid to lie down. "Let's get a little closer to the fire," she said. "I'm cold."

"Me too," said Righteous.

Annie had just closed her eyes when she heard a soft rustle in the woods. "What was that?" she said, sitting up.

"I don't know," said Righteous, hastily pulling her blanket over her shoulders. "What did it sound like to you?"

"Something moving . . ." whispered Annie. The hair on her arms prickled and she could hardly swallow. Righteous moved closer to her. "Annie," she whispered, "look, over there at the edge of the clearing. Do you see something?"

Annie peered into the darkness. Then she, too, saw it. A pair of red eyes watched them, the look unblinking and steady.

"Oh, Lordy," said Righteous, pulling her blanket over her head. "It's gonna' get us!"

The eyes came nearer and a low shape eased towards them. As Annie watched, frozen with fear, the thing drew closer and closer. Just when she thought her brain would explode, the thing came into the light.

The possum waddled out into the light, her babies clinging to her tail like tiny, naked mice. For a moment she stood blinking in the firelight. Then, nose twitching, she turned and disappeared into the woods.

Annie let her breath out with a rush and fell backwards. Righteous stuck her head out from her blanket just in time to see the possum waddle out of sight. "Oh, Annie!" she cried. "Oh, Annie!"

They laughed until their sides hurt then fell asleep and awakened with the first bird call.

The next few days they arose early, traveled during the day and rested in the evening. They rode easily through pine forests where the ground was carpeted with brown needles that muffled the horses' hoofs. Brooks rushed from deep caverns in the earth and bubbled to the surface in clear, cold streams. And hearts-a-poppin' bloomed in the hollows.

Birdsong was bright. They heard the call of the wild geese as they flew in v-formation across the sky. And once, on a moonlit night, they saw wild swans flying against a silver moon.

As they traveled, Annie found herself remembering more and more things. As her eyes grew sharper and she became aware of the way of the woods, she saw signs. Half-forgotten things came back to her, things she'd been taught by her mother and by *Nanye'hi*. Annie found the signs that had been left by others on the trails;

secret markings telling of danger, a small stick figure carved on a tree, a pile of stones that told of a safe place to sleep. The Indians had their own road signs and their meanings were hidden from other eyes.

One day, Annie and Righteous entered a grove of beech trees that were golden and translucent. Annie turned to Righteous and placed her finger over her lips. Pointing ahead, she showed Righteous the remains of a village. Vines grew thickly in the tops of ancient apple trees and the remains of gardens were outlined by fallen fences.

"It's like the *tallahassee*," said Annie. "You can almost hear the people who once lived here."

Overhead, the sky grew dark and thunder rolled through the hills, its sound echoing from hill to hill. The wind freshened, sending clouds scudding across the sky and bending trees and bushes to the ground.

"We've got to find shelter!" said Annie, the wind blowing her hair and whipping the branches overhead. "Let's ride a little farther, maybe there's a cabin where we can wait out the storm."

Uncle William had told her that often new settlements were built near the site of old ones. She was hoping they'd find a cabin still standing that would offer them shelter. The first drops of rain began falling and in a few minutes, they were both soaked. Annie's boots were soggy and squishy and her hair was plastered to her head. A raindrop trembled on the tip of Righteous' nose and she shivered in the cold.

Then, a few yards away, they spied a cabin nearly hidden in a sheltered cove. Only the wind, blowing the branches of the trees, revealed its presence. It wore the lonely look of all empty houses, as though it were waiting for someone or something. No smoke curled from the chimney and the windows were shuttered and dark. But a flower bed near the doorway, where a few late roses still bloomed, showed that someone had recently lived there.

Cautiously, they approached the cabin. There was a lean-to tucked away in the trees. Inside, were two stalls and the hay was still fresh as though it had been recently stored. Leading the horses inside, they fed and watered them. Then, when the animals were cared for, the girls made a dash through the rain for the cabin.

They ran up the wooden steps and stood on the front porch. As Annie reached to knock on the door, she saw the faint markings over the lintel. They would have been overlooked unless you knew what you were looking for and how to read them.

"This is a Cherokee house," she told Righteous, pointing out the markings.

"It's like Moses tellin' the people to mark they houses," said Righteous, "when the angel was gonna' passover."

Annie's heart was pounding as she reached for the latch.

"Maybe we'll be safe here," she said. At her touch, the door swung open and they stepped into the gloomy room.

After the noise of the pelting rain and the wind, the cabin seemed especially quiet. In the dimness, they saw that on the hearth was a small pile of logs and a basket of kindling. Quickly, they looked up into the loft and at the kitchen on the back of the house. All was quiet. But there were still quilts on the bed and pans in the kitchen.

Near the fireplace was a settle and in front of it, a brightly-colored rug. In one corner, a child's rocking horse moved gently in the draft from the door.

"Lock the door, Righteous," said Annie, scrambling in her pack for matches.

"It sure looks like these folks left in a big hurry," said Righteous, drawing the latchstring inside and making the door secure. "Didn't even get to take they things."

"They were probably running ahead of the patrols," said Annie. "Still, nothing's been bothered. I don't think the soldiers have come this far up into the hills."

In a few minutes, the fire was crackling and popping, making a rosy glow against the cabin walls. Later they hung their wet clothes to dry near the fire. They ate sweet potatoes baked in the coals and for the first time in many nights, slept under a roof.

Chapter Twelve

Soldiers

The morning sun, stealing through the shutters, touched Annie's face.

"Wake up, Righteous," she said, sleepily. "We've got to go. The soldiers might be on the way."

After a quick breakfast, they put out the fire and began packing. They'd leave the cabin just as they'd found it, with no trace of their having been there. Then, while Righteous packed their bedrolls, Annie went out to the lean-to to see about the horses. She led them down to the stream that bubbled clear and bright in the hollow at the back of the cabin. Tethering them so they could crop the tender grass, she went back to get Righteous. As she got close to the cabin, she paused, listening.

It was too quiet. No birds sang. She felt a kind of unease, as though something were about to happen. Back inside, she grabbed her things and was turning to leave when she heard a noise outside that turned her blood cold.

"Righteous!" she whispered, ducking beneath the window and peering out through the bottom slat of the shutter, "Something's out there!"

Righteous tiptoed over to the front window. There was movement through the trees. Someone was coming. "Oh, Annie," she said. "I think it's soldiers! And they're coming this way!"

Crawling along the floor to where the rug lay, Annie said, "If this cabin's like my mother's, there's a room. . . ." She flipped the rug back to reveal the trap door. "Quick, Righteous!"

Then, lifting the door, they began throwing down their bed rolls and blankets. Annie looked around the room. Had they left anything? No.

Righteous nearly fell down the steep ladder in her hurry to get down to the root cellar. Then, Annie remembered the door. "The front door!" she said. "Did I lock it back when I came in? If it's locked, they'll know someone is in here!"

Bent nearly double, she ran for the front door, saw that the latch was off and then crawled back to the trap door. The sound of hoofbeats was louder. The soldiers were coming up to the front of the cabin! Grabbing for the ladder, Annie nearly fell on her head in her haste to get downstairs. At the last minute, she reached up to pull the door shut after her. Then, she opened it up again and pulled at the rug to cover the door.

The cellar was pitch black. Feeling their way, Annie and Righteous moved as far away from the opening as they could, easing along the walls to the farthest corner of the room. It smelled of herbs and roots and damp earth. Righteous moved ahead. She made a tiny squeak as her hand brushed against a cobweb.

Overhead, there was a pounding of footsteps on the porch. They could hear voices but couldn't make out the words. Annie reached for Righteous's hand and held on tight. Please, please make them go away, she prayed silently, please don't let them find us.

The footsteps moved closer and grew louder. The soldiers were directly overhead. Annie closed her eyes. She could hardly breathe. Her heart was pounding so hard she could feel it beat in her throat . . . ker-thump, ker-thump, ker-thump.

She couldn't tell how many soldiers there were. She thought only three but she wasn't sure. Footsteps moved across the room and stopped. A soldier was standing directly overhead!

Scarcely daring to breathe, the girls listened as the soldiers thumped away. Then, one of them returned.

"There's no one here," said a voice. "They haven't been gone long, though. The ashes are still warm. . . ."

"Let's go," said another man. Footsteps sounded loud and harsh as the men moved across the room and out the door. Then, there was a thumping as the men went down the steps. In a minute, all was silent.

Slowly letting out her breath, Annie whispered, "I think they've gone."

"Let's wait a minute," said Righteous. Then, turning to Annie she said, "Annie! The horses!"

"They're down in the hollow," said Annie. "I don't think they could see them." They looked at one another in the dim room.

"I want my mama," said Righteous. "I hate this!"

"Me too," said Annie. Then, listening hard, she moved toward the steps. "We've got to get out of here. They might come back."

Out front, Annie kneeled in the dewy grass and checked the hoofprints of the horses. "It looks like they've gone back the way they came," she said. "I think we've got a head start."

They saddled up the horses and headed back up into the hills. Annie thought about the possibility that there might be other patrols looking for Cherokees, but she didn't say anything to Righteous. No need to scare her any more than she already was. They'd been really lucky. Maybe their luck would continue.

Chapter Thirteen

Broken Tooth Gap

The sun was almost directly overhead when Annie took out the map to check their path. Even though there had been no sign of soldiers, she and Righteous wanted to get as far away from the cabin as fast as they could.

"I believe they was lookin' for a family," said Righteous. "Not for us."

"I 'spect so," said Annie, "but if they'd found us down in that root cellar, they'd have taken us back anyway." Checking the map, she said, "Righteous, the valley's not far. Let's ride on and rest there."

They had followed the path of War Woman Creek to the higher mountains, and were now nearing the place that Uncle William had marked on the map for them. In the mountains surrounding the valley there was a gap that the Cherokees called "Broken Tooth." It was there that they were to meet Will Thomas.

They rode for another hour. As they traveled higher in the hills, the air grew cooler. The sun, shining through the brilliant gold and scarlet of the leaves made it seem as though they rode through rainbows. At a small rise, the trees parted and they were on an overlook, an outcropping of the mountain. Dismounting, they looked out over the valley, which spread out before them in all its glory.

"Oh, Annie," breathed Righteous. The valley was washed in gold. The surrounding hills glowed with color and a bright stream sparkled in the sunlight. Off in the distance, the mountains shimmered in a blue haze.

"We're almost home," said Annie. Her heart was full with the look of her land.

"I didn't know mountains looked like that," said Righteous. Before she'd actually seen them, she'd pictured mountains in her mind as sharp things sticking up in the air. But these mountains were rounded and gentle, their tops rolling like waves in the sea. And what Annie had said was true. The mountains seemed to smoke, to tremble in blue haze.

"We'd best go," said Annie. "We've still got to cross the stream."

Later, as they neared the stream and heard the water rushing over rocks, Righteous said, "Let's eat on *this* side of the water." Rocks, smoothed by time and water, were round and white. The clear water rushed and tumbled over large boulders and made whirlpools and waterfalls.

"Fine," said Annie, relieved that Righteous had suggested it. She too, was afraid to cross the swiftly rushing waters. On the map, the stream hadn't looked nearly so large.

While they spread a blanket and set out their lunch, the horses cropped the grass near the water's edge. The valley was sun-warmed and fragrant. High overhead, a few clouds were scattered like sheep across the pale blue sky. Sitting cross-legged on the blanket, Righteous reached up and untied the bag of money from around her neck.

"It gets heavy," she said, rubbing the back of her neck where the cord had rubbed a rough place. "I'm gonna' put it in my pack. We're not gonna' meet any soldiers now. And by tomorrow, we'll be with Mr. Thomas."

When they had finished their lunch and had drunk from the clear, cold stream, they were ready to make the crossing. Packing up their things, they mounted the horses.

"Let's go!" said Annie. "It won't get any easier if we wait."

Annie was halfway across the stream when she heard a strangled cry. Looking back over her shoulder, she saw Righteous's horse move sideways, nearly losing his footing. His eyes rolled wildly as he struggled to keep his balance. The waters rushed swiftly by him and Righteous was fighting to keep her seat.

He's stepped in a hole, Annie thought, as her own horse struggled through the water. "Hang on! Righteous!" she cried.

Righteous grabbed her horse around the neck and clung to his mane with both hands as she tried to steady him. He nearly went down but fought valiantly. Her saddle slipped sideways and as the water rose around his rump, the horse went deeper into the frothy stream. The pack tilted, then slipped.

"Annie!" cried Righteous. "The pack! Get the pack!"

Urging her horse forward, Annie tried to move ahead, to reach the pack before it drifted into the middle of the stream. But her own horse wouldn't be turned. He rose out of the deep water and struggled up onto the bank.

Righteous righted herself and her horse finally gained his footing as slowly, slowly, he moved out of the deeper water and towards the edge of the stream. The pack bobbed like a small dolphin down the middle of the stream until it finally disappeared under the water. The girls watched helplessly as the pack, with its precious content of gold coins, disappeared from sight.

Annie and Righteous lay in the grass, exhausted. It had all happened in a matter of minutes but Annie felt as if it had taken hours and hours.

"It's all my fault," mourned Righteous. "All the money's gone and it's my fault."

"No, it isn't," said Annie. "It's not anybody's fault. Your horse stepped in a hole. He couldn't help it and neither could you." Sitting up, she took off her boots and poured the water out of them. "I sure hate to put these wet things back on," she said, wrinkling her nose. They're squishy."

Righteous looked like a half-drowned mouse. Her hair was curled in wet ringlets all over her head and her clothes were soaking wet.

"You're gonna' catch cold," said Annie, rummaging in her pack for the blue dress that Aunt Martha had first given her to wear. "Put this on," she said. "You're gonna' look kind of dressed up, but at least you'll be dry."

"I reckon so," said Righteous, going behind a tree to change clothes. "Sometimes it seems like nuthin' goes right," she said.

When the horses had rested, the girls readied themselves for the journey. They had to climb the mountain trail that led to Broken Tooth Gap. There, they would spend the last night of their journey before meeting Mr. Thomas.

"This time tomorrow, we'll be safe," said Annie, smoothing the blanket under the saddle.

"I hope so," said Righteous. Then, she asked the question that had been worrying her ever since the pack disappeared. "Annie, what we gonna' use for money?"

Annie shook her head. "I don't know. And I don't want to think about it."

"You mad at me! I knew it!" said Righteous.

"I am not!" said Annie. "I just don't know what to do and I don't want to think about it! We'll have to tell Mr. Will we don't have any money. Maybe he'll let us have some supplies and we can pay him later. But right now, I CAN'T THINK ABOUT IT!"

Righteous was silent on the way up the mountain. It had been a long day and a bad one and she wanted her mama. And even though Annie had said that she wasn't mad with Righteous, in a way she was. She knew that it wasn't Righteous's fault about the pack. Still, the money was gone. She felt angry and ashamed that she felt angry.

The gap on the side of the mountain was easy to see. It really did look like a giant, broken tooth, its edges rough and uneven. It was a passageway that led to the other side of the mountain. And on that other side was safety and after that . . . home!

The girls made camp on an outcropping on the mountainside overlooking the valley and the hills. After they had gathered twigs and pinecones, they built a fire and sat with their backs against the side of the granite outcrop, looking out over the hills.

The sun was setting and the mountains were blue and purple and edged with the sun's rays. There was such a glory on the land that it seemed as though God had traced the edges of the mountains in gold and painted the hollows and the valley blue, then sprinkled the heavens over them with golddust. Annie caught her breath at the beauty of it and Righteous gazed as though she couldn't see enough of it.

Annie turned to Righteous. "You're my best friend in the whole world," she said.

"And you're mine, Annie Rising Fawn," said Righteous.

The next day, Annie and Righteous moved up the narrow path that led up the side of the mountain. As they entered a copse of beech trees, a deer suddenly emerged from the shadows and stood perfectly still, looking at them. She was the color of the tree trunks, pale and creamy. The girls halted and waited. For a moment, the deer gazed at them with liquid eyes then, with a bound, disappeared into the woods.

A little while later, Annie caught a movement out of the corner of her eye. Her horse paused, his flesh rippling. Annie held out a hand in warning to Righteous. A leaf fell silently and caught in Annie's hair. Then, a horse and rider appeared as though from nowhere.

"I've been watching for you," said Will Thomas, smiling.

In a high bed whose sheets smelled of lavendar and sunshine, the girls fell sleep, sinking into a feather tick that billowed around them like a cloud. The last thing Annie remembered was Mrs. Thomas covering them with a patchwork quilt that had all the colors of a rainbow, and was made in the familiar "Indian War Bonnet" pattern.

Chapter Fourteen

The Magic of the Rock

Annie awakened to the mouth-watering smell of hot biscuits. She looked over at Righteous who had burrowed under the covers. "Wake up!" she said. "I'm starvin!"

Dressing quickly, they went into the kitchen where Mrs. Thomas was setting the table for dinner. They had slept all night and through breakfast. Mr. Will was standing near the hearth and next to him was the tallest man Annie had ever seen. He was Cherokee and wore traditional dress of buckskins. His gray hair was braided with the soft down of swans' feathers and around his neck was hung a brass gorget, a kind of medallion on which was carved the figure of an eagle.

"This is my father, Chief *Yonaguska*," said Mr. Will. Annie and Righteous curtsied, as they'd been taught to do. Just then, Mrs. Thomas called them to dinner.

Mrs. Thomas was short and plump, like a little pigeon. She wore her hair in a bun that was constantly slipping to one side. "These girls must be starved," she said, bustling around as she put the food on the table. "Now, come on, all of you. Everything's hot!"

Halfway through dinner, just as she was buttering another sweet potato biscuit, Annie remembered about the money. How could she have forgotten? Suddenly, she lost her appetite. She put the biscuit back on her plate.

There seemed to be a lump in her throat that the food wouldn't get past.

Righteous, who'd been telling the chief about how Charity was going to come join them on Star Mountain, looked over at Annie. Their eyes met. Righteous quit talking.

"Well, you girls *surely* aren't through eating," said Mrs. Thomas, when both girls refused more chicken and dumplings. "You haven't eaten enough to keep a bird alive!"

Righteous, when she thought no one was looking, slipped two biscuits off the plate and put them in her pocket. Later she told Annie, "I figured we might need 'em."

Annie knew she had to tell Mr. Will about the money. When the dishes are done, she told herself. The girls helped Mrs. Thomas in the kitchen, then when everything was put away and tidy, they went back into the parlour.

"Annie," said Mr. Will. "You and Righteous come with me. We'll go over to the store and get the supplies you need. I'll help you choose so you will have the provisions you need to carry you through the winter."

This is it, Annie thought miserably. I have to tell him about the money. And, to her surprise, she burst into tears.

After drying her tears and listening to Annie's story about the lost money, Mr. Will said, "Now, Annie. Did you really think we'd let you go without? Don't you worry about it. Everything will look brighter when you're home again. We have a gracious plenty here, and we want to share." His eyes were the color of smoke and were kind.

Mrs. Thomas held out her hands to the girls. "Come

on, now," she said. "Let's go see what we need." She led the way to the store, which was connected to the main house by a breezeway. Out in the chicken yard, Plymouth Rock chickens scratched at kernels of corn.

In the store, bolts of brightly-colored material lined the shelves. Nearby were barrels filled with flour, corn meal and other grains. Tables held different kinds of furs; racoon, fox, and rabbit as well as the hides of deer. Indian pipes and a basket piled high with pigtail twists of tobacco sat on the counter. There was a drop for mail and messages, and maps on the wall tracing the trails leading to and from New Echota and Ross's Landing.

Taking down several bolts of cloth, Mrs. Thomas told the girls to choose what they wanted for dresses. "Come spring, you'll be pretty as flowers," she said.

Righteous chose a cloth of pale yellow with tiny pink roses while Annie picked out a pattern of white with blue flowers. In a tiny voice, Righteous said, "Please. can I get some for my mama? She'll be here soon and she can make our dresses."

"Bless your heart," said Mrs. Thomas. "Of course you can. How about this one? It's my favorite. I love the butterflies." And when they were through, Mrs. Thomas rolled the cloth neatly and tied it with string. "I want to send some seeds to *Nanye'hi*," she said, carefully pouring the seeds of "clove-pinks," and honesty plant into twists of paper. Then from her supply of spices, she counted out three nutmegs, two cinnamon sticks and a precious packet of cloves, things that were precious and hard to come by.

"I know that *Nanye'hi* will have most things in her garden," said Mrs. Thomas, "but these things are rare." Finally, when everything had been chosen there were bags of flour, sugar, oil for the lamps, salt, and thread.

The girls' things had been packed and the supplies were ready to be loaded onto a pack mule. Annie hadn't re-packed any of her treasures. She wanted to show her turkey-feather coverlet and her rock to Mrs. Thomas.

Annie took her rock and coverlet and went into the sitting room. Twin settles faced one another in front of the fireplace and rag rugs lay scattered on plain wooden floors. Geraniums grew in pots on the window sills and there was a spinning wheel in one corner. Mrs. Thomas was reading aloud the translation of St. Matthew that had been made by the Reverend Worcester and printed at the *Phoenix* printing press.

Chief *Yonaguska* sat by the fire, listening.

> For I was an hungered, and ye gave me meat:
> I was thirsty, and ye gave me drink:
> I was a stranger, and ye took me in:
> Naked, and ye clothed me: I was sick,
> and ye visited me: I was in prison, and
> ye came unto me.

When Mrs. Thomas finished reading, Chief *Yonaguska* sat looking into the fire. "That seems to be a good book," he said. "But it is strange that the white people are not better, after having had it so long."

Annie sat at the chief's feet. She was holding her rock and had been telling him about her sunflower room on the mountain. As she talked, she turned the rock towards the flames, watching as tiny sparks glittered in the light.

"What do you have there, Annie?" asked Mr. Will.

"I'm not sure, sir," she said. "*Nanye'hi* left it for me. I think it's magic but I don't know how to make it work."

"Let's see," he said, stretching out his hand. He

looked at it, then getting up, went over to the lamp on the table. Holding it close to the light, he looked at it for a long time. "Oh, my goodness," he said softly. He looked over at the chief who went to join him. A moment later, Mr. Will laughed softly. "So, Annie. You don't know how to make it work?"

For a minute, Annie thought he might be teasing her. "Nossir," she said. "It doesn't do anything."

The chief laughed too, then he said, "Come. We'll tell you how to make it work."

Annie stood next to them. "It's gold, Annie," said Mr. Will. "Pure gold. *Nanye'hi* has given you magic. The earth's magic. You don't have to worry about losing your coins anymore. You and Righteous and Charity and *Nanyi'hi* won't want for anything."

Annie was astounded. How had *Nanye'hi* found the gold? Had someone given it to her? Somehow though, she knew she'd never know the answer. *Nanye'hi* would simply look at her and go about her business.

"Mr. Will," she said, "Will you take care of it for us?"

"That I will, Annie," he said. "You know, under the new laws, Indians are not allowed to own gold or even to dig it on their own lands. But this is old gold and was a gift. We'll see that you and the others are well paid for it. I don't know what it's worth, but it will be enough to keep you from worrying for awhile." He held the rock in his palm and lifted it toward the ceiling. "It's the earth's gold, treasure, and reward. It's like your sunflowers, Annie, touched by the sun and holding its essence."

Chief *Yonaguska* went back to the settle and took out his pipe along with a deerskin pouch filled with tobacco. He held out the pipe for the girls to see. "It is sacred," he said. The red stone of the bowl was carved into the shape of a tortoise and the stem was covered with a shiny snakeskin. Annie handed it back to him and he packed it with tobacco. Touching a piece of straw to the fire, he lit the pipe. He blew the smoke towards the ceiling, in the direction of the sun. Then he blew the fragrant smoke towards the four corners of the room; the four directions of the universe and the four corners of the earth. He called upon the spirits of the Grandfathers, asking for their blessings for the Cherokees and for the people who wept for them.

As the blue smoke drifted in the quiet room, the old chief closed his eyes and said a special prayer for the girls and for those they loved.

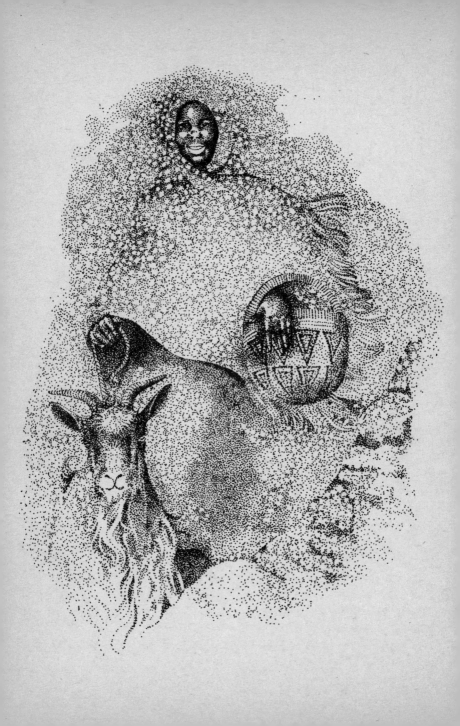

Chapter Fifteen

Return to Star Mountain

The rooster crowed the girls awake just before dawn. The sky was the color of a pearl when Annie awakened. She had butterflies in her stomach. Today was the day! She looked over at Righteous who was pretending to be asleep.

"Righteous," she said, "we're going home to Star Mountain!"

After a breakfast of eggs, sausage, and biscuits, they were ready to leave. They said their goodbyes to Mrs. Thomas and to the chief. Led by Mr. Will on his spotted Appaloosa horse, they rode out into the soft morning light. Chief *Yonaguska* and Mrs. Thomas waved goodbye from the front porch.

The air grew cold as they rode higher and higher up into the mountains. Fir trees were thick and fragrant and held beads of moisture like tiny pearls in their springy branches. Annie remembered the ride down the mountain when she and Uncle William had ridden to New Echota. It seemed like a long time ago.

Righteous was worried about her mama. Had she left New Echota yet? As she rode up the mountain path, she wondered what lay ahead for her. She was going to a place she'd never been before and was calling home. It was Annie's home but would it be her home too?

Shadows were stealing down the side of the mountain when they approached the path leading to the cabin. Annie could hardly breathe, she was so scared. What if *Nanye'hi* weren't there? What if the cabin was empty and cold? What if the sheep were gone, and the chickens? What would they do? Where would they go?

They rounded the curve in the path. Up ahead, Annie saw the cabin. A plume of smoke rose from the chimney, and through the shutters a lamp glowed. Then, the front door opened and a slender figure stepped out onto the porch.

"*Nanye'hi!*" cried Annie, getting down from her horse and running up the path. "Oh, *Nanye'hi*, I've come home!"

That night, Annie sat in her father's old rocking chair, gazing contentedly around the familiar room. Sweet herbs hung from the rafters and her mother's loom stood in its corner. Sweet potatoes were baking in the coals. Firelight danced on the walls and glowed on her father's dulcimer, which held the wind in its strings. Home, she thought drowsily, Home at last.

Over the next few days, Annie and Righteous explored every inch of the place. Annie showed Righteous the sheep and the sheep barn and where her sunflower room used to be.

"We can do it again," said Righteous, walking around the square.

Annie shrugged, "I don't think so," she said.

They picked wild grapes, the sweet green scuppernongs whose skins were thick and flecked with gold. They ate so many their lips itched. After the first really heavy frost when the earth was silver, they picked ripe persimmons and *Nanye'hi* made jelly that was pink and sweet. She showed them how to make pumpkin bread and then took them down to the meadow where the bee skeps held dark, sweet sourwood honey. And they waited for some word from Charity. But none came.

By November, the leaves had fallen from the trees and lay in silken mounds and you could see the inside of the hills through the bare trees. Once in a while, a visitor would come to the cabin, having been told that it was a place where shelter and food could be had. Some Cherokees had escaped the beginning of the long trail to the west and had made their way up into the mountains. Once in awhile, there would be word from those on the trail but they had no word from Uncle William or Aunt Martha.

Each day, Righteous waited for her mama. Soon, snow would fall and the narrow trail up the mountain would be impassable until spring. Charity needed to come soon.

With the onset of winter, the cabin grew more isolated. Overnight, gray clouds covered the tops of the hills. The cabin seemed lost in mist and lonely. Frozen dew coated the tops of the fir trees and the sheep huddled close in the barn.

Annie and Righteous went out to the front porch. Their breath made clouds on the air. Lifting her head, Annie took a deep breath. "I smell snow," she said.

Righteous burst into tears.

"What's wrong?" Annie asked, alarmed. "How come you're cryin'?"

"My mama cain't make it up this ol' mountain in the snow," wailed Righteous. "I'm never gonna' see her again!"

"Oh, Righteous," said Annie. "Yes, you will. She's gonna' show up any day now. Why, she'll have Joshua and everything will be fine. She said she'd find you no matter what, and she will!"

But Righteous was not to be consoled. She turned and went back into the cabin. "I hate this ol' mountain!" she cried. "It's not my home and I hate it!"

Annie went into the barn and closed the door. There was the sweet smell of hay and the warm scent of animals. As she milked the cow, she thought about Rumblegumption and how the cat used to slip into the barn at Uncle William's and wait for a squirt of fresh cream. Annie put her head against the cow's warm side and fought back tears. She missed that silly cat and wondered what had happened to her. And she missed Uncle William and Aunt Martha. She wished Charity would come soon.

Righteous came around the corner of the cabin, her arms piled high with small logs. As she started up the front steps, she felt the first snowflake touch her cheek. She looked up, tasting the feathery softness of the snow.

Annie came out of the barn and, putting the milk bucket down, closed the door. She wrapped her shawl around her shoulders and started back to the cabin. Snow was beginning to fall tenderly. She looked through the gentle whiteness and saw something moving at the edge of the path.

At the same time, Righteous looked out and with a squeal of joy, dropped the logs and started running.

"Mama!" she cried, "Here I am! It's me, Righteous!"

Charity stood in the path, a basket over one arm, a rope held in one hand. The snow began falling faster, coating the dark shawl she wore over her head and dusting Joshua's coat with a feathery lightness.

Later, *Nanye'hi* brought in hot tea and honey and sat in the rocking chair near the hearth as Charity explained how she'd finally made her way to Star Mountain. Righteous sat as close to her mama as she could get while Annie sat on the floor holding Rumblegumption who had made the long journey in the basket that Charity had held over her arm.

"The Frierson's are white friends of Mr. William's," said Charity, taking a sip of tea. She told them that the Frierson's, who were part Scottish, had left New Echota for North Carolina. "They said they didn't want to stay in a place that was so soaked with misery. Miz Frierson said it was too sorrowful."

"Where did they go?" asked Annie, who felt Rumblegumption's purring running through her body like a warm coil.

"To a place called Grandfather Mountain, north of here," said Charity. "They've got folks there. They brought me as far as Mr. Will's. Then he brought me the rest of the way. When it started snowing, he had to get back less'n he got stranded up here. But by then, I was nearly over Jordan," she said, nodding her head. "Nearly over Jordan."

"I'm sho' glad you home, Mama," said Righteous.

"I'm glad to be here," said Charity, looking over at *Nanye'hi*. "I just wish Mr. William and Miss Martha could have come, too. Yo' son, Mr. William, is a fine man," she said, her eyes filling with tears. "They went with the others on the trail. The soldiers, they came and closed up the house. They took the animals and some white folks were planning to move right in. Miss Martha, she was real sad but she say the Cherokees is her people now and she was goin' where they go."

Nanye'hi gazed into the fire. "To the darkening land," she said softly.

"I reckon so," said Charity.

Snow continued to fall all night, blanketing the cabin and rounding the tops of trees and covering the path. In the warmth of the barn, Joshua made herself at home. And in the warm and cozy cabin, the new family members settled in for the night.

Chapter Sixteen

When the Roses Bloom

Spring came to Star Mountain. The yellow rose that Annie planted near the porch sent out tiny green shoots. Baby chicks hatched and tottered around the chicken-yard like bits of yellow fluff. Lambs were born. Joshua made herself at home and seemed to be confused as to whether she was a sheep or a goat. In the hollows, purple violets scented the air with a wild, cool fragrance.

One evening, just at twilight, Annie was sitting on the porch listening to the chorus of peepers, tiny tree frogs no bigger than her thumbnail. A bob-white called from the garden with a mournful cry. "Bob-white, bob-white, bob-white," came the clear, two-note whistle. The call was followed by a three-note call, the scatter call . . . "Where-are-you? Where-are-you?"

Annie rose from the steps and looked out towards the grove of trees at the end of the garden. It was not a real bob-white that she'd heard. The bird never gave the scatter call with the spring call. No, what she'd heard was someone calling.

A tall figure emerged from the trees, moving as silently as a shadow. In his deerskin shirt and trousers, he blended with the tree trunks and in the soft light, was barely visible.

Nanye'hi came out onto the porch and looked out.

113

"This is a safe house," she said to the young man. "Welcome."

Over a meal of fish and grits, the man told them news of the trail. "It is being called '*nunna-da-ul-tsun-yi*'," he said, "the trail on which they cried."

The man, who was a mixed-blood named Sam Butler, had a brother who had been in charge of one group on the trail. "He told me of a man in his company who lost his entire family to death," he said, looking over at *Na-nye'hi* as though to ask her permission to continue.

She nodded. "We must know. The girls need to know too."

"This man wrote from Missouri," said Sam Butler, "to tell us that it was very, very bad." From his pouch, he took out a piece of paper that had been folded and re-folded many times. "I will read you what he says:

> Womens cry and make sad wails. Children cry and many men cry, and all look sad when friends die. But they say nothing and just put heads down and keep on go towards West. Many days pass and people die very much.

He pushed his plate away, his food barely tasted.

"Many of our people have died on this trail. Mrs. Ross died on the way to the Arkansas."

Annie looked up. She couldn't believe it. The beautiful Mrs. Ross? How could that be? Had she too, been forced to march?

Sam Butler told them about the long chain of Indians that stretched from Kentucky to Illinois. "Sometimes women could not stop long enough to bury their children."

Annie looked over at Charity who sat crying but making no sound.

"We don't know how many have died. But there is a trail of graves and a trail of tears from Georgia to the Arkansas."

For a moment, no one spoke. *Nanye'hi* went over and stood at the window, looking out at a sky that was thick with stars. Annie and Righteous moved closer to Charity. The room seemed filled with unspoken words and unwept tears.

Two months after Sam Butler told them about the "Trail of Tears," Mr. Will delivered a letter to the cabin. It was from Uncle William in Arkansas.

> We are well and send our love. Our people still suffer. We have taken unto us two children who were orphaned on the trail. They are boys, one eleven years and one five years of age. We miss you and love you. I hope by now that Charity has made her home on Star Mountain. I send my love to my mother and to each of you.

Annie and Righteous would live many years on Star Mountain. And they would have many adventures and many joys. They had escaped what would be known forever as "the trail on which they cried." They would be forever changed because of it.

Each spring, when the yellow rose bloomed fierce and sweet, they would remember the others and would keep the memory in their hearts.

About the Author

Sara Harrell Banks was born in Tuscaloosa, Alabama, and raised in Savannah, Georgia where she now lives. She is a journalist and a poet and has written a number of books for children and young people and a novel for adults. Her love for the Cherokees came as a gift.

Remember My Name is by way of thanks.

Afterword

One hundred and sixty years after the Trail of Tears, the Reverend Samuel Worcester, along with his friend and fellow missionary, Dr. Elizur Butler, have been remembered by the State of Georgia. Illegally imprisoned for protesting the seizure of Cherokee land, Worcester and Butler have been posthumously pardoned by Governor Zell Miller.

Seven generations of men in Samuel Worcester's family had been ministers. So it was natural that the young Samuel was drawn to Andover Theological Seminary where he studied Latin, Greek, and Hebrew and where he became an expert in linguistics. Before his father became a minister, he was a printer and Sam had worked at his father's press as a "printer's devil," setting type and running errands. After college, Samuel's love of words and language were part of the reason that he would find his way to the Market Street rooms of the Board of Foreign Missions in Boston. When he was assigned to the Cherokee Nation, his first goal was to learn the Cherokee language, the syllabary invented by Sequoyah only a few years earlier.

At New Echota, the Cherokee capital, Samuel met Elizur Butler, who brought medical training along with missionary zeal. The two young men were enthusiastic and completely caught up in the cause of the Cherokee

Nation. Worcester began work at *The Cherokee Phoenix*, the first Indian language newspaper. He was also translating the book of St. Matthew into the Cherokee language, and keeping the Board of Foreign Missions posted on the missionary work in progress.

But the good will of the missionaries was no match against the corruption of the state politicians and the infamy of Andrew Jackson. Georgia had already decided that the Indians had to leave their land. Senator Lumpkin believed that the reason for the stubborness of the Cherokees in refusing to move was the "religious fanaticism" instilled in them by the missionaries. Governor Gilmer agreed. Gilmer persuaded the state legislature to enact a law requiring all white persons living in the territory to obtain a license from the governor—the license to be had by taking a loyalty oath to the State of Georgia. Eleven missionaries refused to take the oath. The case of the controversial eleven was heard before the Gwinnett County Superior Court. All were indicted and released on bond, pending trial in the State Supreme Court.

Worcester returned home to New Echota where his wife, Ann, was recovering from the difficult birth of their daughter, Jerusha. But he was informed that he would be arrested again if he remained at his home. Reluctantly, he left his family and crossed the border into Tennessee to await his September trial. But on August 14, his daughter Jerusha died. He hurried home but was too late for the funeral. The Georgia Guard, anticipating his arrival, arrested him for trespassing on Georgia soil. On September 15, all eleven men were sentenced to four years' hard labor for supporting the Cherokee people and refusing to take the loyalty oath.

Gilmer, serving his last months in office, was aware of

public sympathy for the missionaries. He didn't want them to become martyrs in the eyes of the public. He sent word that all would be pardoned if they would either take the oath of allegiance to the state or leave its boundaries. Nine of the eleven took advantage of the offer and left the state. Only two, Worcester and Butler, refused. They served sixteen months of their sentence before a new governor freed them.

One hundred years later, Marian Starkey, telling of the Cherokee civilization said of their imprisonment: "That one act of courage makes the whole world braver."